Science fiction magazine from Scotland

ISSN 2059-2590
ISBN 978-0-9934413-9-4

Shoreline of Infinity is available in digital or print editions.
Submissions of fiction, art, reviews, poetry, non-fiction are welcomed:
visit the website to find out how to submit.

www.shorelineofinfinity.com

Publisher
Shoreline of Infinity Publications / The New Curiosity Shop
Edinburgh
Scotland
050317

Contents

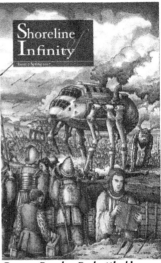

Cover: *Reader Embattled* by
Steve Pickering

Editorial Team

Editor & Editor-in-Chief:
Noel Chidwick

Art Director:
Mark Toner

Deputy Editor & Poetry Editor:
Russell Jones

Reviews Editor:
Iain Maloney

Assistant Editor & First Reader:
Monica Burns

Copy editors: Iain Maloney,
Monica Burns, Russell Jones

Extra thanks to: Caroline
Grebbell , M Luke McDonell,
Chris Kelso

First Contact

www.shorelineofinfinity.com

contact@shorelineofInfinity.com

Twitter: @shoreinf

and on Facebook

Pull up a Log

Last summer at an Event Horizon here in Edinburgh, Jane Yolen, SF poet extraordinaire and writer of many books enthralled an audience of writing students. We were therefore delighted when she agreed to talk to our Poetry Editor Russell Jones for this issue of *Shoreline of Infinity*. You can read about her thoughts on poetry, her strong female characters, YA fiction and writing being about "tell the True". And better—we share four of her poems, dear reader, for you to hear her distinctive voice call out to you. We at the Shoreline of Infinity yurt are looking forward to Jane's return visit to Scotland in the summer.

Arrival was the best SF film of 2016; no arguments, thank you. Last week I finally read the source—Ted Chiang's short story: *Story of Your Life*. It showed once again how a short science fiction tale can be, at its finest, a condensed explosion of ideas, character and story. A quick Tweet brought a list of other short stories adapted for films (thanks folks!), from *Sentinel* for *2001: A Space Odyssey*, to a tweet pointing out that Philip K Dick stories saw many transformations into films.

So Nolan, Spielberg, Wachowskis, Zemekis and all, I hope you've subscribed to Shoreline of Infinity—your next blockbuster film could be right here in your hands.

Noel Chidwick
Editor-in-chief
Shoreline of Infinity
March 2017

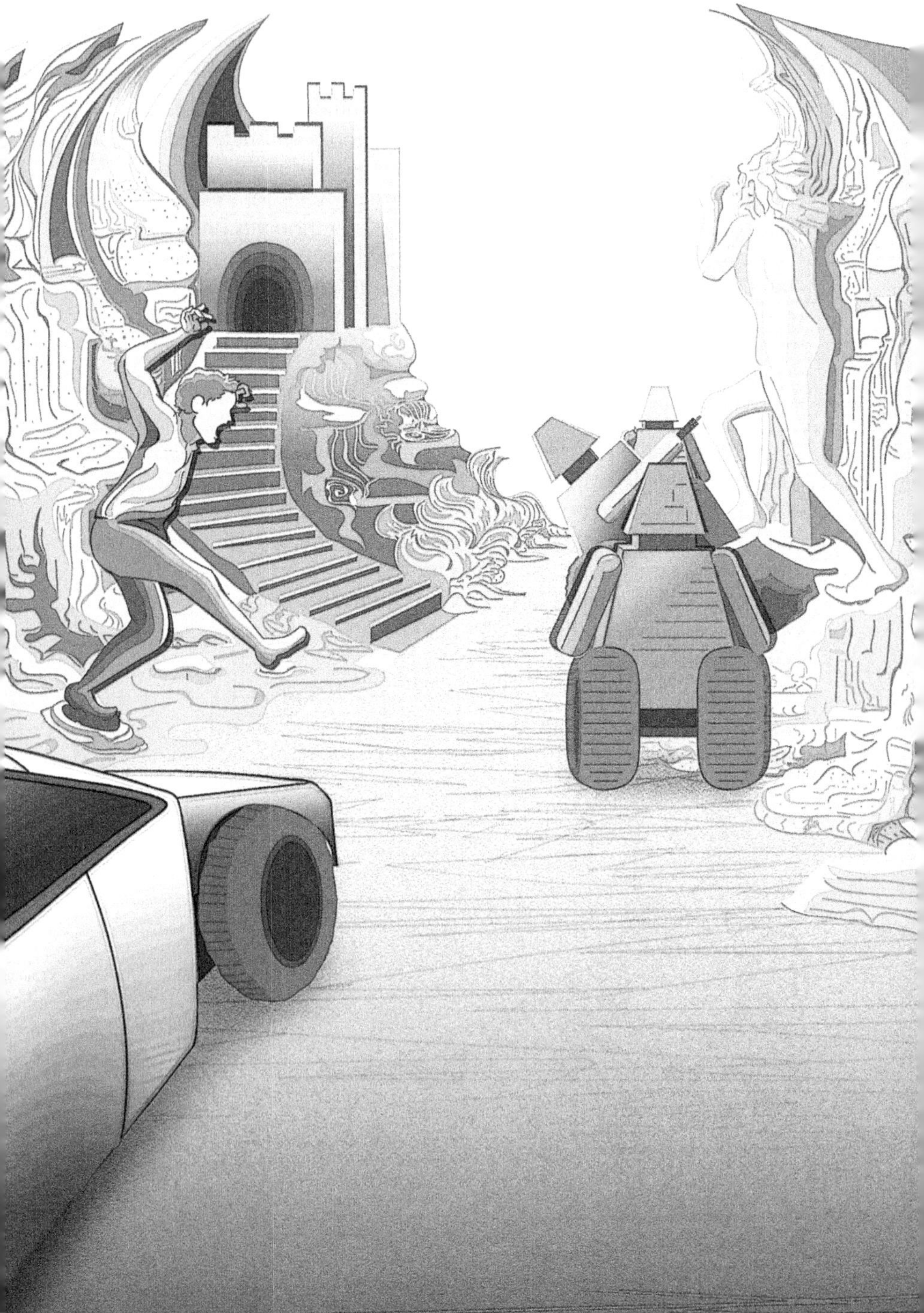

The Walls of Tithonium Chasma

Tim Major

Art: Jessica Good

Halliday pauses at the window that curves around the loading bay of Tharsis Foxglove. His bare arms reflect the pale red of the sky. The nicks and cuts on the window, the result of dust storms, are a complex net.

Are the sculptors really still out there? He imagines the three of them, free of the suffocating atmosphere of the base. Working, or just patrolling the surface aimlessly. It would be difficult to blame them if they never returned.

He continues along the curved passageway, moving away from the living quarters and the rest of the team. It seems unreasonable, stashing the aye-ayes out here beside the trucks and rovers in the workshop. He traces a finger along the lockers, counting up. Ai403, Ai404, Ai405 absent serving in the chapel, Ai406. Should they have given them names? People had, with the early models, back home. But they had been companions rather than tools.

The moulded faces gaze back at him from within shrouds of dustproof sheeting. Naked as the day they were born. At the touch of a panel, Ai407 slides out, suspended by the armpits on two extending rods. Some way to sleep.

What's the hold-up? The boot process gets slower each time. The aye-aye's smooth mask twitches. The corners of each empty eyepit flicker with fine motor calibrations. It feels intrusive, watching an aye-aye wake. Halliday keeps still to allow its recognition software to kick in.

"Bring a trundler to the doors," he says, "I'll meet you there."

Ai407 moves away, its smooth feet padding softly on the shop floor.

Once he has suited up, Halliday slides himself into the passenger seat of the trundler. Ai407 does not turn to watch him as he struggles to arrange his legs into a comfortable position.

"Let's go."

The aye-aye raises both of its handless arms. Each stubby end glows blue as it interfaces with the onboard navigation system. The hatch door of the workshop rises silently and then they are outside.

Copper-coloured storm clouds have gathered in the distance, beyond the Valles Marineris. Other members of the team have talked about seeing clouds like these in dreams. They say that their dreams are more vivid, these days. Halliday himself doesn't dream, or doesn't remember.

He turns to look at the closed bay. The hatch is invisible from outside, fitted flush to the curve of the building. Behind the loading bay the spokes and bubbles of the living quarters emerge only slightly from their protective hills of dust. The buildings are sculpted from the same dull red as the Martian rock beneath.

"There's no chance the storm will head this way?" he says.

"There is a chance," the aye-aye replies.

"Quantify."

"Six per cent."

They travel in silence until they reach the end of the dirt track from the base. Halliday realises that he has always thought of it as a winding driveway, as if the base is a country house on Earth. They should sculpt a row of trees to line the edges of the road, do the job properly. The trundler slows to a halt.

"Where is our destination?" the aye-aye says.

"I don't know yet." Halliday fishes the screen from the pocket of his suit and unrolls it on his lap. It displays a map, preprogrammed by Aitchison in logistics. The base is marked in green and their own position is a throbbing orange dart. At a point five times the distance they have travelled hangs a parallelogram outlined in black. Its edges shift constantly. "Somewhere between F4 and F7, west of Tharsis Fuchsia. Get close and we'll take it from there."

The ground is rougher here. Halliday lurches to one side, pushing against Ai407's slick shoulder to right himself.

"You're not from the chapel, right?" he says.

"No. Ai406 and below service the chapel."

Halliday nods. A decade ago most colonists would have been horrified at the thought of religion thriving on Mars. When the Foxglove council had displayed the blueprints for the chapel sculpture, the reaction back home had been one of polite disgust.

He looks outside as they push through the first of the half-pipes that lead to the plains. Its sculpted walls are perfectly smooth. Only the upper edges are frayed, where the regolith has been scooped and shifted by the wind.

He glances at the moving shape on the screen. "Hey, aren't you all on the same network? All of you aye-ayes, and the sculptors?"

"Yes, we share bandwidth."

"Aitchison says there are three missing. They left last week to begin sculpting the new storehouse, west of here. Can you hear them?" He slides a finger along one of the blades at the edge of the map to reveal Aitchison's brief. "They're models SC33 to 35."

Ai407 turns its head as if straining to listen. "They're out on the periphery. I can barely feel them."

"They've been out there for days. What are they doing?"

Ai407's smooth lips move before speaking, as if rehearsing a response. "Sculpting."

Once they have crossed the sculpted bridge that connects Foxglove to the other regions, they emerge onto the plains proper. The sunlight, though filtered through the cloud of red dust and the tinted windscreen, stings Halliday's eyes. He feels a sense of freedom at seeing the bare rocks that litter the desert to either side. They are unsculpted, unchanged, unchanging. Tharsis Foxglove will never extend this far and yet they are still close enough that no new base will be constructed here either. This space will remain preserved, an area of natural beauty, or perhaps natural ugliness.

The trundler finds a smooth route. The jolting lessens.

"Stop here." Halliday pushes his way out of the vehicle and kneels, one gloved palm on the ground. The regolith is hard and compacted. It must have been pressed flat by the sculptors.

Back in the passenger seat he says, "Keep to the same route they took. Should prevent us from hitting any dead ends."

They reach a rise. From here Halliday can see the smoothed route winding west around the boulders. It is less direct than seems optimum. He remembers Sunday outings on his father's motorbike, to Ullswater and beyond. His father would say, "Never take the direct road when there's a scenic route in the offing".

The trundler gathers speed as it sweeps downhill. The parallelogram on the screen shrinks.

"We're closing in on their location." Halliday watches as the shape dwindles to a point. Soon, it is replaced by three faint blue specks in a cluster.

"Hey, stop. We've overshot them somehow." He looks out of the rear window. The desert is vast and light. None of the boulders are large enough to hide a sculptor.

He jabs at blades onscreen, pulling up the brief and then the nav calibration. He swings open the door and clambers up onto the roof of the vehicle. From here he can see that the terrain ahead is not as blank as the desert behind them. A dark ripple crosses the horizon. A canyon. The sculptors must be somewhere below them.

"How close are we to Ius Chasma?" he says.

"The nearest tributary canyon is one kilometre from here, directly ahead."

"Keep driving. Follow the road." Halliday has never ventured as far as the Valles Marineris, despite the proximity of Foxglove to some of the canyons. He looks down. Without being conscious of it, he has buckled his restraining seatbelt.

At the mouth of Ius Chasma the smoothed route takes a dogleg turn. The trundler stops at the summit and Halliday stares into the depths of the canyon. The rock walls are more orange than red.

"The road continues downwards," the aye-aye says.

"Take it," Halliday says.

The descent is giddying. The sculptors have only flattened an area wide enough to allow themselves to return without obstacle. The right caterpillar tread of the trundler runs on rougher ground, close enough to the edge to make Halliday grit his teeth.

"They're scheduled to be way east of here," he says, trying to distract himself. "Equidistant between Foxglove and Fuchsia, that was the council brief for the storehouse. And they haven't even started building. What the hell are they doing down here?"

The aye-aye pauses before answering. "Sculpting."

They reach the floor of Ius Chasma. Halliday wipes his forehead with the arm of his suit. The trundler lurches from side to side. The smooth road now winds in tighter turns than before.

"Forget the road," Halliday says, "Just follow its general direction."

The right wall of the canyon is a steep hill of rubble. It must be the result of landslides. Sunlight plays on the wall to the left of the trundler but the floor is in shade. Halliday glances down at the screen. The three dots are to the east, close. He sees the Foxglove bridge arc above. They have backtracked to arrive beneath their earlier route. These canyons criss-cross more than he realised.

"We are entering Tithonium Chasma," the aye-aye says.

Until now the walls have appeared fractured and rough. Here, their surfaces look as smooth as the sculpted road. A light swirl of ash dances ahead of them. Red-hued light blooms from a semi-circular passage.

Ai407 turns its blank face towards Halliday.

"What's that look for?" he says. "Carry on, that way." He points ahead, then pulls his hands under his thighs. He feels suddenly conscious of the aye-aye's own stubby limbs.

Red light bathes the trundler as they enter the passage. Before Halliday's eyes have adjusted to the light he hears a noise that is tinnier than the hum of the motor. It sounds like a mouse scratching below floorboards.

The walls of Tithonium Chasma are pillar-box red. The canyon is enormous, as if this is the true Martian surface and everything above is mountainous.

He sees the squat, tractor-like sculptors immediately, even though they are dwarfed by the rockface. One of them scratches at the right wall of the canyon. A cloud of dust rises around its suction funnel. The other two are facing away from the trundler as if surveying the work of their colleague.

Halliday peers up at the walls. Breath fogs the inside of his helmet, clearing from the top down. First he sees a sculpted stone bicycle that leans against a boulder. Further along the canyon, stepping stones dot a stream with static, sculpted wave crests. A young boy is frozen mid-leap with just the tip of one shoe touching rounded stone.

He cranes his neck. Standing apart from the canyon wall is a structure that towers above him, somehow too large for him to have noticed straight away. It is a steep hill with more stone waves lapping at its base. On top of the hill is a sculpted building with sheer sides that reflect the red light. Its towers are almost the height of the canyon walls.

He senses Ai407 standing beside him. The aye-aye is staring upwards at the wall where the sculptor is still at work. Here, the rock has been carved into less representative forms. It takes Halliday several seconds before he sees that it is the enormous figure of a man. His body is distorted, bent forward into a loping run. Flames surround his head like a lion's mane. His mouth is wide open and twisted in agony.

"Jesus," Halliday says. His voice is little more than a breath, "What is this?"

He flinches as Ai407 says, "It is a nightmare."

"But who the hell has nightmares like that?"

The aye-aye shields its eyes.

"I do."

※

Halliday forces a smile as Reverend Corstorphine steeples his fingers and settles into his chair, which is the only fully complete item of furniture in the chapel. Though the structure of the building was completed a month ago, backlogs at the Sandcastle sculpting foundry have delayed the pews. Only a hanging tapestry smuggled from Earth interrupts the bare white walls. It is embroidered with the words, 'The sky above proclaims his handiwork'.

"I have long suspected as much," Corstorphine says. The chair creaks.

"That they have nightmares?" Halliday says.

Corstorphine chuckles. "Your sons and your daughters shall prophesy, and your young men shall see visions, and your old men shall dream dreams."

Halliday wishes that there were a desk to separate them. "Except the aye-ayes aren't sons and daughters, or men, young or old."

In the opposite corner of the chapel, beside a tea tray on the floor, a kettle comes to the boil. Corstorphine crosses the room and bends to fill two mugs, handing one to Halliday. "It's only instant, I'm afraid."

Halliday accepts the mug and wishes he hadn't. He would prefer to take nothing from Corstorphine. People like him charge interest on a debt, however small. Before he knows it, he'll be given chapel duties like the rest of the team. He had been rash to approach the Reverend with his findings. It had been a moment of weakness.

Corstorphine sips his drink noisily, then rests the mug on his belly. "Dreams are only echoes. Expressions of an experience not fully processed. The dreams are not the thing. Tell me again what you saw."

Halliday describes the scene at Tithonium Chasma again. It is easy, as he has thought of it often in the days that have passed. The boy in the stream, the castle, the burning man. What can it mean?

When he finishes, he rubs his face. He has drunk the coffee without realising it. "It's a vision of Earth, that much is clear. And, as far as I know, Foxglove's aye-ayes were constructed back there, then shipped over with the rest of us. But that doesn't really explain anything. What do you make of it all?"

"Well. I'm happy to say that it supports a pet theory of mine," Corstorphine says. "I must thank you for coming to me with this information."

Smug bastard. Halliday resents the bait but takes it anyway. "What's your theory?"

The Reverend's eyes travel upwards. Above him is only a prismatic white space.

"That the aye-ayes possess souls."

✳

After Halliday awakens it, Ai407 stands loose-limbed in the centre of the workshop. Sleepy and sulky. It waits for him to speak.

"Who is your father?" Halliday says, finally.

Ai407 doesn't answer.

Maybe he phrased the question badly. He bends to look into Ai407's sunken eyepits. "Who is your AI template?"

The aye-aye replies instantly. "Felix Ransome, the son of Professor Elias Ransome."

Halliday gasps. "*The* Elias Ransome?"

"Professor Elias Ransome."

So these aye-ayes were among the first on Mars, or at least their AI subroutines were. All this time, Halliday has been working alongside antiques.

Back on Earth, twenty years ago, Elias Ransome had been a key player in aye-aye technology. He worked for years, developing faster and more efficient chips and behaviour routines. But the true breakthrough wasn't an issue of computing power. Ransome bestowed on the aye-ayes the gift of imagination.

Aye-ayes were technically advanced, but in practical terms they were imbeciles. Give a man a fish and you feed him for a day; teach a man to fish and you feed him for a lifetime. Teach an aye-aye to fish and it'd bring you shoals and shoals, fine. But give it a single fish without also providing clear instructions and it would just stare at the fish for a lifetime. What was missing was imagination, and Ransome provided it. Or rather, his then eight-year-old son, Felix, donated it via an imprint of his brain patterns.

Halliday waves to dismiss Ai407. The aye-aye clambers back onto its plinth and arranges its short arms so that its weight is supported by the extended rods. As the rods retract, carrying the aye-aye backwards into the housing, Ai407 turns its blank face towards Halliday. Halliday shudders. He glances at the rows of aye-ayes in their sarcophagus-like closets. They are all on the same network. They are family. They are all little Felix Ransome's children, able to function only because they had once been inspired by his gift for invention and his developing moral code.

Their blank faces seem less inert. Halliday sees the subtle flinches of sleep.

✳

Reverend Corstorphine makes a show of being engrossed in his book. Halliday enjoys the idea that perhaps he is reading the Bible for the first time. All of the clergy here are amateurs. They are only appropriating religion in response to market demands.

"You don't believe it yourself," Halliday says.

Corstorphine glances down at the book, for a moment misunderstanding what Halliday is referring to. He removes his spectacles, which have pinched craters into the bridge of his nose.

"I wouldn't have returned," Halliday says, "But I can't let you go on like this. It's a farce." There are now only a handful of the team, including himself, who still do not attend Sunday services. From overheard conversations in the canteen it is clear that recent sermons have been filled with talk of the aye-aye's souls.

The Reverend's neat goatee is a dark smile beneath his lips. "I merely repeated what you yourself told me."

They stand side by side to look through the scarred window. The chapel is at the highest point of Tharsis Primrose. They can see over the sculpted barriers to the crescent-shaped sand dunes that shuffle slowly across the Martian plains.

"And the trips to Tithonium Chasma?" Halliday speaks slowly to prevent his voice from cracking. "You encouraged the fools to take those pilgrimages, too?"

"Your colleagues have simply found meaning in an astounding phenomenon. It is comforting to know that God speaks to the aye-ayes as well as to us."

Halliday's shoulders slacken. "I think I understand. You assert that God rules the aye-ayes. So then, if we ever do find life out there, we can assume that God's the boss of them too. Everyone and everything answers to Him. Right?"

He sees Corstorphine's raised eyebrow reflected in the window.

"It's blindness," Halliday continues. "You're showing God's work where there is none, only engineering. You're encouraging these people to ask the wrong questions and find the wrong answers, just to promote your faith." Annoyed at his own lack of restraint, he changes tack. "When did you leave Earth? Ninety-seven, eight?"

"Yes. Ninety-eight."

"And you're smart enough to have read the small print during sign-up. We all donated. Straightforward scanning and uploading of our brain patterns for potential use in templating." A hollow laugh. "I bet the idea appealed to you. Providing moral guidance to the aye-ayes."

Like Corstorphine, Halliday had been at school in the eighties, back when 'aye-aye' equated to merely 'vacuum cleaner' or 'cook'. Then there had been a miraculous leap in their capabilities at the end of the decade, due to the brain-pattern breakthrough. He remembers the TV shows. Aye-ayes on obstacles courses, aye-ayes flying planes. There was much talk about the march of technological progress. It was the stuff of dreams and school projects.

Halliday retrieves a screen from his jacket pocket and unrolls it on the lectern, ignoring Corstorphine's protests. He pulls up an image browser and, after a minute's search, turns the screen towards the Reverend. The screen shows a photo of a blunt, high-walled castle on top of a hillock that spirals upwards from the sea like a snail's shell. "There. That's the building I saw in Tithonium Chasma."

"I know it," Corstorphine says. He sounds fascinated, despite himself. "That's Lindisfarne Castle."

"It was," Halliday says. "It's just rubble now. Did you know that Elias Ransome died there during the war?" He shudders, remembering the news-report images of the firestorms after the bombs. Flames and flesh.

The Reverend's face shows recognition of the name. "And the boy in the stream?"

"Felix Ransome, of course. All those things were his memories, expressed by the aye-ayes through the sculptors. They all share bandwidth. Felix Ransome witnessed his father's death and then he relived it in his dreams. So the aye-ayes do too."

Streaks glisten on Reverend Corstorphine's cheeks. Embarrassed, Halliday busies himself rolling up the screen. "Tell me again that you believe the aye-ayes have souls."

Corstorphine runs his fingers along the edges of the lectern. His hands stop shaking. When he looks up again, his eyes are cold. "We all require mysteries. The colonists do."

"Not mysteries. Lies."

✳

In the days and weeks that follow, Halliday approaches nobody. Even once the enthusiasm for pilgrimages to Tithonium Chasma has diminished, the congregation accept the sculptures as proof of the all-encompassing purview of God. Halliday spends his free time alone in his cabin.

He does not only think of Felix Ransome. Halliday donated his own brain patterns twelve years ago, just like Felix, just like all the other would-be colonists. Aye-ayes inspired by his thoughts may still be in service, somewhere on Mars. And if they are, might they not dream his dreams, just like the Foxglove aye-ayes dreamt Felix's?

Except Halliday doesn't dream. This in itself makes the prospect more fascinating to him. What would his aye-ayes, if they exist, tell him about himself? He dredges his memories for moments that might hold up against Felix's firestorms. The early death of Yvonne, his sister. The late death of Constable, his dog.

He must know which of his memories defines him.

Time passes. He makes some calls.

✳

Four years later, a contact of a contact is finally able to help. Halliday is directed towards the remote outpost of Wigwam in the Iani Chaos region. His transfer request takes months to be processed and is met with incredulity by the authorities. While the Tharsis region is as bleak as anywhere on Mars, at least there are people there.

Not only does Iani Wigwam contain no human employees, the small base houses no humanoid aye-ayes either. In the workshop there are only rows of sculptors with their suction funnels neatly recessed into their blunt bodies. The single AI processing unit is a white, cuboid block that crouches in the centre of a tiny control room. It hums like a fridge. It has no auditory receptors and no input panel. Halliday stands before it and wonders whether this white box really does hold the blueprint of his brain pattern. Whether it thinks as he thinks. Whether it dreams his dreams.

His only function is to assess and repair the sculptors. It is the first such intervention in a decade and is barely needed; the sculptors are capable of performing many of the repair tasks themselves. He sleeps, reads novels, and maintains the sculptors and the exterior of the base. He waits.

After three weeks, without warning or ceremony, the processing unit sends a silent command to one of the sculptors. Halliday is asleep when it leaves through its low catflap door. Lacking a trundler, he pulls on his suit and follows on foot.

He wanders among the mesas and hillocks of Iani Chaos. Some of the flat-topped blocks are so tall and thin that they could be Earth skyscrapers.

While he walks he reviews the events of his life. He orders and ranks the images. He remembers the time he believed, for an hour or so, that one his girlfriends had shot herself. He remembers becoming lost in the forest near to his house and spending the night beneath the stars. He remembers another girlfriend and the loss of his virginity. He remembers his parents and his friends. He remembers deaths. Bodies piled upon bodies.

He heads away from the distant bump of Iani Wigwam. The terrain underfoot is hard rock so there is no evidence of the sculptor's tracks. He chooses directions at random. He is prepared to explore the area all day in the hope of finding the sculptor.

At a sandy junction between mesas, he sees traces of tyre tracks. They continue south and meander from side to side between the rock outcrops. They are wandering just like he is wandering, as if pre-empting his steps.

They are his. The steps, the AI fridge, the sculptors. Perhaps he and they identify so strongly that they can even predict where he will walk.

A bulky shape appears ahead. Halliday has to squint to see that it is not natural rock. As he approaches he recognises that it is a sculptor.

He groans. The sculptor is tilted to one side and its bulky chassis appears warped. Has it sunk into soft ground? No, beneath the dust layer the rock seems firm. The suction funnel is low to the ground. It had been in the process of hoovering up the regolith, ready for it to be reconstituted as sculpture.

But what was it sculpting before it became trapped? Did this sculptor dream his dreams?

He skirts around it, keeping it at arm's length in case of serious malfunction.

The rear panel of the sculptor hangs open at ninety degrees. It must have been mid-way through compressing and carving the regolith. Halliday bends to examine the object that lies on its side within the tray.

It is a tulip with cupped petals half-open.

He reaches out to touch it. The tulip is cold and hard. It means nothing to him. If he dreamt, he would not dream of tulips. He would dream of…

But the only images that occur to him are of aye-ayes and sculptors. Sculpting, dreaming. His obsession, for years now. His life.

He notices that there is something peculiar about the machine. On closer inspection the chassis appears totally off-kilter. It is a distorted caricature of its usual appearance.

Hesitantly, he places a hand on the chassis. Instead of metal he feels cold, pressed sand.

He begins to weep.

This is not a sculptor, but a sculpture.

Tim Major's time-travel thriller novel, *You Don't Belong Here* (Snowbooks) is available now, as are his two novellas, *Blighters* (Abaddon) and *Carus & Mitch* (Omnium Gatherum). His short stories have featured in *Interzone* and numerous anthologies. He is the Editor of the SF magazine, *The Singularity*, and blogs at www.cosycatastrophes.wordpress.com

A review of *You Don't Belong Here* is available on the Shoreline of Infinity website.

AN INFINITE NUMBER OF ME

Dan Grace

According to Grandma my mother first died when I was twelve. I'll admit I didn't notice at the time, but with hindsight I can spot the changes. She stopped taking sugar in her tea. I had presumed she was on a diet or that her chronically sensitive teeth had finally worn her down. She dressed a little differently too; more colour, wilder, a little more free. I was outwardly mortified, but secretly pleased. I'd always thought her choice of clothes a little drab. And she was certainly around more, picking me up from school most days, despite my protests.

"Things have slowed down at work," were her words.

We weren't close. Up until that point I had been more or less raised by my Grandma. I didn't resent it particularly. Mother was a clinical, sharp woman, as befitted her profession. Many of my friends had much more interesting and convoluted family situations than me. 'Dad' had never been more than an abstraction or an object of confusion; something other people had that I understood in principle, but couldn't see the precise purpose of.

Mother had been immensely practical when it came to having a child. The facts of my conception were laid out before me as soon as I was deemed old enough to understand their meaning. Sperm donation from a series of suitably excellent candidates, egg screening at the most advanced and, therefore, expensive clinic.

"I chose you darling. From all the available options, I picked you. Doesn't that make you feel special?"

It did. Although, in a childish way, I sometimes wondered what happened to those she didn't choose.

✻

Despite these changes she still lived for her work. She was a genius, or close to it, according to Grandma. According to many people. She had sailed through school and university. A female physicist is still a rare thing, in all places it would seem, and she made capital from that fact.

I remember one particular tearful episode. I was eight, or maybe nine. Mother was late home again. She'd promised to be back in time for dinner and I, unwilling or unable to understand the importance of her work, had unleashed my full fury at poor Grandma. Undaunted, she reared up at me, finding those extra inches the elderly seem to lose as they go about day-to-day tasks, finger pointing, wattle of skin below her chin quivering with anger.

"You listen here young miss, you understand this. Your mother cares the world about you. She would do anything for you. Do you understand? What she's doing, her work, she does it for you. So we'll have no more of this. Am I clear?"

She was very clear. My young mind couldn't fully understand that there were things greater than my need for a mother at the dinner table, but I knew I was wrong.

✻

I've tried to read the papers she published, but they make no sense to me. They don't get to the heart of her work anyway. All that stuff is under lock and key somewhere.

Art is my thing, my gift. I paint, people buy it, praise it. It makes me happy. That's enough, isn't it?

My work is very public, maybe too public I feel sometimes, the polar opposite of my mother's. She wasn't a shy person by nature, but she would never talk of work, of where she worked, of who she worked with. I understood that it was important. That was enough.

Wasn't it?

※

The defect remained though, a microscopic spanner in the works, and it took her from me again when I was only fifteen. I saw it that time, although I didn't know what it was that I saw. The changes were more noticeable, the differences greater. Coffee, not tea. Alcohol in the house for the first time. Clothes all too similar to what I was wearing. And a renewed need for contact, for my company, that only infuriated my teenage self.

"Why are you behaving like this, Mother?"

"Behaving like what darling?"

"Just, you know, following me around, texting me constantly. I mean, just leave me alone."

"But I love you darling. I just feel so lucky to have you. That isn't so bad, is it?"

"Ugh. Mother."

"What darling?"

And so it went.

I still saw a lot of Grandma. She quizzed me endlessly about my mother. Her behaviour, her habits, any changes in mood.

"Why are you asking me these things, Gran?"

"What do you mean?"

"I mean why are you asking me about mother? You've noticed she's changed too haven't you?"

"I don't know what you mean darling."

"Gran."

"I think maybe it's the pressure at work. That's all." She smiled. "Nothing to worry about. Nothing to worry about at all."

And I didn't worry really. I was a teenager. Teenagers don't worry about their parents for the most part, they have enough of their own problems, real or imagined, to deal with.

✳

Mother died for the third and final time on the day of my eighteenth birthday. The day I became an adult. Just like that. She left for work and never came back. A car accident. Utterly random.

I was numb. I was hysterical. I was inconsolable.

I realised that I hardly knew her, that I was just on the cusp of being able to get to know her.

Yet I carried on.

I went to university.

I went a little crazy.

I moved to London, inevitably.

I made a name for myself.

I had a succession of nice, but ultimately pointless men.

I missed my mother.

✳

"It's like this." Grandma bent forward in her wheelchair and scooped up a handful of gravel from the path.

I'd asked her about mother, about her work. It was more out of lack of anything else to say than any hope I might hear something new. We'd spoken of it a thousand times before. Grandma enjoyed talking of her genius daughter.

She held out her frail, translucent hand to me, filled with pebbles and bits of twig, clods of dirt. It shook gently as she spoke.

"Each of these stones is a person, the same person give or take a few minor details."

She hefted the handful high into the air and we watched them splash down into the pond.

"The ripples that spread from each are their lives. Those points where they touch, they interfere with one another, you can feel. That inexplicable feeling of serenity that strikes you when you least expect it, at the oddest moments. Where our lives touch. An infinite number of me, an infinite number of you. All just ripples on the pond's surface. That's how your mother explained it to me. I mean your real mother."

"Gran?"

"Oh I'm sure there was more to it than that. When they recruited her she said she couldn't talk about it anymore, not even to her own mother." A small smile. "But she did. Sometimes. If they touch, we can see into them, she said to me. If they touch we can travel between them."

"Gran I don't understand what you're saying."

"Your mother, darling. She drove a hard bargain. They needed her and she knew it. She was brilliant. There was nothing they could do about her condition, about her heart, but she got insurance. She made them promise."

"Promise what, Gran?"

"That if she died they'd bring another her through."

✳

I watch the light through the leaves on the old oak. My hand traces the creases in the bark, fingertips brushing lichen and moss. The sun is good on my skin. It soaks through my pores, down though muscle and bone, into the marrow. I feel lifted, inexplicably alive, and I know in this moment that my sister, one of many sisters, is near.

I wonder if she knows her mother. Our mother. Or if, like mine, she too disappeared one day. An empty space left behind. A hollowness that always had been there, muted, but now pushed to the fore.

And as the feeling passes, as it always does, I long to reach across the radius of the ripple, to see her, for her to take me in her arms and for her to tell me that everything is going to be okay.

Dan Grace lives in Sheffield. His novella, *Winter*, is published by Unsung Stories and was reviewed in Shoreline of Infinity 4. The review is also published on our website, www.shorelineofinfinity.com

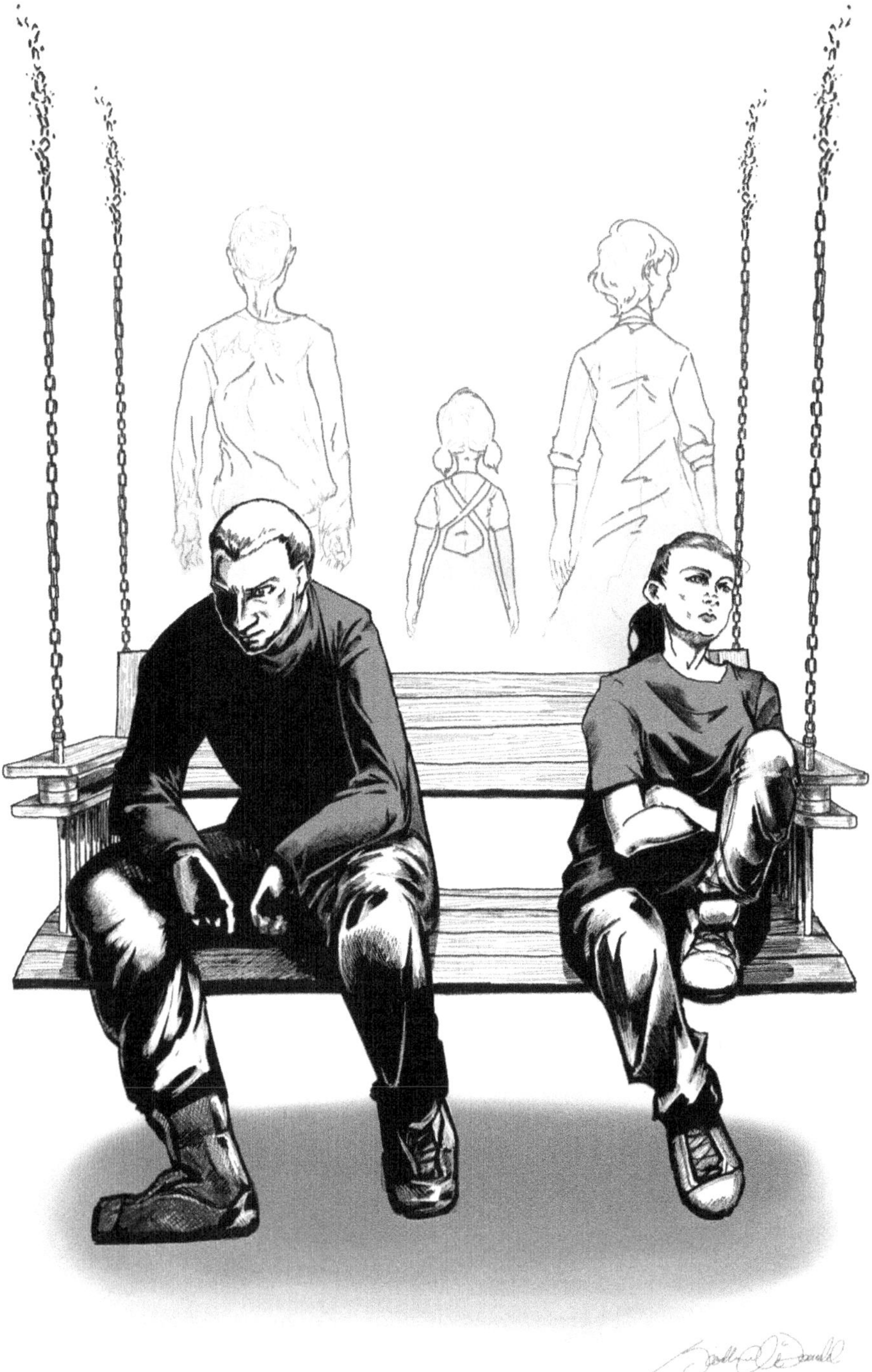

Brother's Keeper

Shannon Connor Winward

Abby (I.)

A human being is not like a bullet. We don't begin with a single act—a finger on a trigger. Our existence depends on the confluence of choice, desire, factors far more complex than angle, range, wind. Even if, in hindsight, our outcome seems inevitable, the trajectory of a life is not so easily calculated.

So, how to avoid an undesired outcome? Where do you start? Not at the end. You have to go back. You have to unravel. But how far? To the bottom of the stairs, the beginning of the breakdown? Further. Before he buys the gun, before he becomes addicted, before the marriage dissolves, before the army. Before the child. Before the first confluence is even crossed. You have to go back to where the lines are clean.

Back to when life was simple.

Jesse

While his mother had her hands stuck inside the turkey, Jesse slipped outside to spark a joint.

The neighborhood was quiet, full of fireplace scents and white chimney smoke. Clearing a thin layer of snow off the backyard swing, Jesse settled on the bench and rocked, enjoying the familiar, rhythmic squeak of the chain.

Then Abigail came around the corner of the house, red sneakers crunching over snow. Thirteen years old now, she seemed to have aged years instead of months since Jesse went away to college. Black *New Moon* t-shirt but no coat, blonde hair dyed black and swept up in a severe ponytail. She stopped when she saw him and put a hand on her hip. "What are you smoking?"

"I'm not."

Abby looked at him with that odd, fierce gaze that had been unnerving him all week. "That's weed. Give me some."

Jesse coughed into his glove. "I'm not giving weed to my baby sis—"

"I'll tell Mom you have it. M-oooom!"

"Shut up! Fine! Jesus."

Jesse felt a qualm as he handed her the joint. He could still picture Abby dancing in pink footie pajamas, brandishing her first lost tooth. "Just take a little. A puff. Not too much."

Blue eyes twinkling, Abby pinched the roach between black sparkly fingernails and sucked it like a straw.

Jesse gaped. "How long have you been smoking?"

"Oh," she said, and held her breath. Exhale. Handed it back to him. "A while."

"Jesus." Jesse took another hit. When he went to pass it back, Abby shook her head.

"I don't have much tolerance in this b—…" She smiled goofily and shook her head. "Mm. Hey. Do you have any cigarettes?"

Jesse pulled the packet of Reds from his coat and handed her one. The lesser of two evils, he figured. Abby smoked the cigarette like a death-row inmate, head thrown back. When she coughed, she giggled, which made Jesse giggle.

Abby brushed off a patch of snow and sat next to him on the swing. "I want to ask you a question," she said. "It's… for a story I'm writing."

"Okay."

She stared at the house as if searching for words in the grooves of the aluminum siding. A sudden breeze blew snow from the roof, a starburst of particles and light.

"Say you had a kid."

"Oh…kay?"

"And… say you found out you were going to die. But. Say someone could make it so that you didn't. Have to die. Maybe."

"What, like… they found a cure?"

"No. I mean… well. I just mean what if someone could fix things? Fix… your life."

"Abs, I don't know what the hell you're talking about."

"I'm talking about second chances, Jess."

Jesse shrugged. "Whatever. Sounds great."

"But…" Abby took a deep breath. "If someone could give you another chance, to do things differently… so that maybe bad things wouldn't happen… it might mean she wouldn't ever be born."

"She who?"

Jesse caught a flash of Abby's eyes, and then she was examining her nails on either side of the still-burning cigarette. "Your daughter." She put her nail in her mouth and chewed it off. Spat, took a drag from the cigarette. Looked at him. "Would you do it?"

Jess laughed. "I'm confused."

"Damn it, listen. If you could live your life differently so that you might not die, but it meant your daughter might not be born, would you do it?"

"I don't know. No."

"No?"

"Nah."

"Why not?"

"I don't know. What do you want me to say? I'm not a father."

"But if you were."

"But I'm not. And people don't get do-overs. This is stupid."

"But say you could."

"How?"

"It doesn't matter."

"What. A time machine? Aliens? A magical doorway?" He was teasing, but Abby wasn't smiling.

"Damn it, Jesse, *how* is not the point."

"Is there something about my future that I should know?"

The cigarette was burning to ash between Abby's fingers. Jesse took it from her, smoked it down to the filter, and crushed it out.

"If I had a kid," he continued, "… even if I could make it so they never existed, somewhere they would have existed. Right? On some… level? Or whatever? Well… you know what Mom always says. Once you have a kid, your life isn't just yours anymore."

He'd been looking at the side of the house. When he looked back, Abby was staring at him. It was getting creepy. "What?"

"So…" Abby whispered. "No?"

Jesse shrugged. "It just wouldn't be right. Right?"

Abby's eyes filled with tears, sparkling like snow-dust before cascading down her cheeks. In the next moment, she was hugging him. Jesse's hands went awkwardly to her back. He hadn't held her since she was small enough to carry.

"Hey, it… s'ok. What's wrong?"

"I'm sorry, Jesse, I'm not a genius. I kind of figured you'd say that. But I hoped… I don't know. I love you."

"I… love you, too?"

Abby disentangled herself and swiped at her runny nose. "I gotta go."

"Okay."

She jumped off the swing and looked at him. She looked way older than she should.

Then, for just a moment, Jesse saw Abby standing on a ridge over a forested valley. She wore hiking gear and a cowgirl hat over short blonde hair, and that was weird. He'd never been hiking with Abby.

The wind kicked up, stronger this time. Abby bristled, her ponytail (black, not blonde) striving to break free from her head. "It'll pass," she said. "It's just the distortion."

"What?"

"You won't remember this part, anyway, but Jess… I only had a few minutes. I didn't know what else to do." She looked like she was about to start crying again, but she turned away. Jesse watched her crunch back to the house. He felt dizzy and sick, like he used to get from reading comic books on long car trips. His head was full of Abby images—Abby in her car seat, sleeping slack-jawed and drooling. Abby in a cap and gown. Abby a grown woman on a mountain top, on a rooftop, in a white room. Abby yelling, crying, staring down at him while the world spiraled, shuttered, faded.

And his own voice, saying things he'd never said.

You're the genius, Abby. All those degrees. Maybe you can figure out how to fix me.

Jesse turned and spat a bad taste from his mouth into the husks of his mother's tiger lilies. The weed was probably laced with something. Fuck.

He hoped Abby would be all right.

He dropped his coat in the hall so Mom wouldn't smell it on him. He should have said something to Abby, too, told her to put on some perfume or something, but when he walked into the kitchen she was there with Mom already. The two of them stood at the counter in matching aprons, smothered in the aroma of roasting turkey and diced onions. They glanced at him before turning back to their work, twin gestures of feminine dismissal.

Jesse plucked a carrot stick from the vegetable platter and bit it in half. "So what's your story about, Abs?"

"What story?"

"The one you're writing."

Abby scooped a handful of cut celery into the big metal bowl. "Well, I'm thinking about this one about a girl who can change into either a vampire or a werewolf, at, like, will? 'Cuz her parents were one of each. And she falls in love with this guy who's a prince from this rival cadre, but she doesn't know it. But I haven't started writing it yet."

"What about the time-travel thing?"

Abby scowled at him. "I don't write time-travel. Sci-fi is stupid."

"What about the thing with the dying, and the kid…?"

Jesse trailed off. He felt nauseous again, like what happened outside, but more of an aftershock than a wave—and with it, another *déja vu* − like memory of something he'd never done. Handing Abby a bundle, tight and warm. It smelled of hospital sheets and powder, and it was somehow the most important thing in the world.

Sierra. For the mountains. And Elizabeth. For Mom.

"Jesse, what are you talking about?" Another clump of celery went into the bowl. "God. You're so weird."

Jesse put the remaining half of the carrot back on the plate. His appetite was gone.

Abby (II.)

Maybe you can figure out how to fix me.

Dr. Abigail Walker rode the shuttle straight from the hospital to her offices at Phalynx Corp. Her com buzzed in her pocket, unanswered. At home, Abby's partner, Michael, would have just learned of Jesse's death.

She inhaled a cigarette as she jogged between the platform and the security terminal. Pausing to deposit the stub in a vacuum slot, Abby caught a glimpse of herself in the vid-feed. Red-eyed, haggard. She'd been keeping a vigil for weeks, fussing over the tubes and monitors, the bioplastic cap sewn over the missing parts of Jesse's brain and skull. All for nothing—she couldn't save him. He'd told her that, his eyes fixed over her shoulder, indifferent, his body a shrug with every induced breath. In the end, the machines cried out for him, the nurses swarmed like pink vultures on his blanketed bones, but it was too late. Her brother was gone long before he became a corpse. He was gone even before he put the gun to his head, that day on the roof of the rehab clinic.

Where did it start? How far back?

All down the long white corridor to her suite, Abby rewound history in her head, looking for a way in. *When*, she wondered. Not *if*—she was reasonably sure she could do it, even if it meant subverting the goodwill of her employer. She'd been playing with the idea for years, even went so far as to submit a research proposal. It'd been tabled for ethical concerns—the long-term effects of temporal displacement on cellular evolution had yet to be determined. But Abby had the resources. She had a treasure-trove of data in her lab and a strand of her own thirteen-year-old hair. (She'd tossed the *New Moon* t-shirt in a box just after the Thanksgiving that Jesse announced he was dropping out of college. For whatever reason Mom had saved it, airtight in a bin in the attic, unwittingly preserving that precious bit of DNA).

Abby swiped her ID card, entered her office, and brought her terminal to life. A photo at her work station caught her eye—Jesse and their mother at the military hospital in Sacramento, where Sierra was born.

Even then, holding his infant daughter, Jesse hadn't been all right. Too thin. A certain look in his eyes. Or was that only hindsight?

On the day of his suicide, Jesse had laughed at her. *You're the genius, Abby*, he'd said. *All those degrees. Maybe you can figure out how to fix me.*

And maybe she could. She could go back. As to whether or not she *should…* she'd figure that out when she got there.

The family photograph zeroed out. Grabbing a data key and her ID, Abby headed for the lab.

Sierra

The little girl had been making birds. Graceful, sweeping shapes that disappeared back into gravy almost as fast as she could carve them with her spoon.

The other children ate their dinners, happy, crammed in around Mama Lucy's glass coffee table. There were cartoons on the big screen. Later, everyone would get a slice of pumpkin pie.

The little girl didn't care about pie. Also she didn't like this cartoon, or this house, and Mama Lucy was not her mama. *Her* mama went to sleep with a needle in her arm and never woke up.

There was a knock at the door and Mama Lucy swished through the family room to answer it. The girl could see the front hall from where she was sitting. She recognized Miss Millie, the lady who had taken her from her house and brought her here. Miss Millie saw her looking and smiled. Mama Lucy smiled too, the way she only did when other grownups came over.

The third lady did not smile. She was tall and blonde, with a face the little girl thought she should know but couldn't think why. Then she realized it was not unlike her own. The little girl felt her heart begin to flutter like birds' wings inside her chest.

"Hi, sweetie." Miss Millie came over to the coffee table. She put her hands on her knees and bent closer, her voice quiet, though everyone in the room was listening. The other kids kept their eyes on the cartoons, forks going up and down into mouths. They were watching with their ears.

"Could you come into the sitting room for just a little bit? You'll be back in time for dessert," she added, as if this mattered. The little girl was already leaving her spoon in the gummy mashed potatoes and rising to her feet.

They led her into the tiny room off the front hall where Miss Lucy kept the dressy dolls no one was allowed to touch. They sat her on the checkered sofa. The blonde lady sat on the chair. Miss Millie and Mama Lucy went into the kitchen for tea.

The lady smelled like cigarettes. Her fingers twitched like she needed one real bad, like the little girl's mother's used to do. "I'm Abigail," she said.

"I'm Sierra. Sierra Elizabeth."

"Yes, I know. I'm your aunt."

Sierra was about to say that couldn't be right—her mother didn't have any brothers or sisters. Then she closed her mouth, not wanting to seem stupid. She'd had a father, once, too.

"Do you remember your dad?"

Sierra shook her head. "Miss Lucy says he died, too."

"Yes." After a while she added, "Sierra…. That's the reason I'm here. I'm your closest relative now. If you want… you can come live with me."

Sierra picked up one of the dolls from the basket on the floor and began to tug its auburn hair.

"When did my dad die?"

"Friday."

Friday? "Why didn't he come before?" Sierra asked, trying hard to sound like she didn't really care about the answer. She'd been living with Mama Lucy for seven months.

"He would have if he could. He was sick."

"My mom said he was a loser junkie."

The lady—Abigail—could have said the same thing about Sierra's mom. It would have been true. But she didn't. Sierra appreciated that.

"It's pretty much the same thing, isn't it?"

"Why didn't you come, then?"

Abigail shifted on the sofa and didn't answer right away. She looked like she half didn't want to be there.

Sierra studied her over the doll's head. "You don't like kids."

"I'm ambivalent about them, to be honest with you." Abigail laughed at herself, obviously thinking Sierra didn't know that word. But Sierra understood a lot of things. Like that this "aunt" wasn't here for Sierra so much as she was looking to do something nice for someone else. Sierra's dead dad, maybe, or the grandmother she was supposed to be named for.

"But it's not that," Abigail continued. "I was hoping things would turn out different. But here we are." She offered a sad smile. "You look like my mom."

"I look like you."

"Yeah, I think you do. They say you're very smart. And artistic. You draw?"

Sierra nodded. "I write stories."

"I used to write too," said Abigail. "A long time ago. I was never good at finishing, though."

"What do you do now?"

"I'm a biophysical engineer. That's a kind of doctor. I design programs that trace back cellular evolution."

"Why?"

"To reverse degeneration… disease."

Sierra thought of her parents. "So you fix people?"

"In theory." Abigail studied her hands in her lap. "Not everything can be fixed."

"At least not by going backwards."

Abigail stared at Sierra. "Right," she said. "Anyway. I work a lot. I don't know anything about raising kids. But I have a nice apartment, and my boyfriend can cook, so. It's up to you, Sierra. What do you think?"

The girl made a pretense of considering it, then dropped Mama Lucy's doll into the basket, head first. "Can we go now?"

Abby (III.)

We do not begin with a single act, Abby thought, struggling to keep her grip on the handhold as the shuttle swayed over downtown, *but perhaps we can be defined by one.*

Lizzie, straddling the middle aisle with all the strength and grace of youth, glanced up from her com and gifted Abby a smile. She was in the midst of her midterm exams at University, necessitating constant earnest conferences with her classmates, but she knew the ride was rough on Abby's arthritic joints.

"Sure I can't beg you a seat, Mom?" she asked, tilting a head towards the benches.

"I'm fine," Abby lied, banishing any hint of pain from her face. Lizzie turned back to the device in her hands, immersing herself once more in the depths of xenolinguistics.

Abby studied the top of the young woman's honey-blonde head, seeing not the tall, confident Lizzie as she was now, but Sierra Elizabeth as she had been, small and strange on that first ride home so many years ago. Sierra with her face pressed up against the window to see the city sprawled hundreds of feet below, the magnificent convergence of lights and steel, the hugeness of a world where she had lost and gained a family in a single night. Beneath the ache in her hand, Abby could still feel the avian frailness of the girl's shoulder as she reached out to hold her, moved by some fetal sense of love.

Was that it? Was that the moment she'd become not-Abby, but a parent? Or had that happened earlier, with the knock on the door at the foster home? When the word "adoption" first left her lips? The night that Jesse died and Abby ripped herself in and out of time, the moment she returned, shaking and vomiting, to her laboratory floor?

Or had it been in motion all along?

"Our stop is next," Lizzie said, taking Abby's hand. "I'm so glad we're doing this. I'm starving. Let's share a plate of tikka masala, what do you think?"

"Absolutely," said Abby, though she had little appetite anymore. The aging process was catching up with her—hardly noticeable for the first few years since her trip back, but now she was dyeing her hair, taking pain meds, treating her skin—it was getting harder to keep Lizzie and Michael from realizing the extent of her degeneration.

To tell Lizzie she was growing old quickly, irreversibly, Abby would also have to explain why. She wasn't ready for that conversation. She knew she'd have to do it, sooner rather than later. But not now. Today was about Lizzie—a special mother-daughter lunch at their favorite restaurant to celebrate the nearness of a bright and promising future. That was how it should be.

The past could come later.

Shannon Connor Winward is an American author of speculative fiction and poetry. Her writing appears in *Fantasy & Science Fiction, Analog, Persistent Visions, Pseudopod,* and elsewhere. Shannon is also an officer for the Science Fiction Poetry Association, a poetry editor for *Devilfish Review,* and founding editor of *Riddled with Arrows Literary Journal.* She lives and writes in Newark, Delaware.

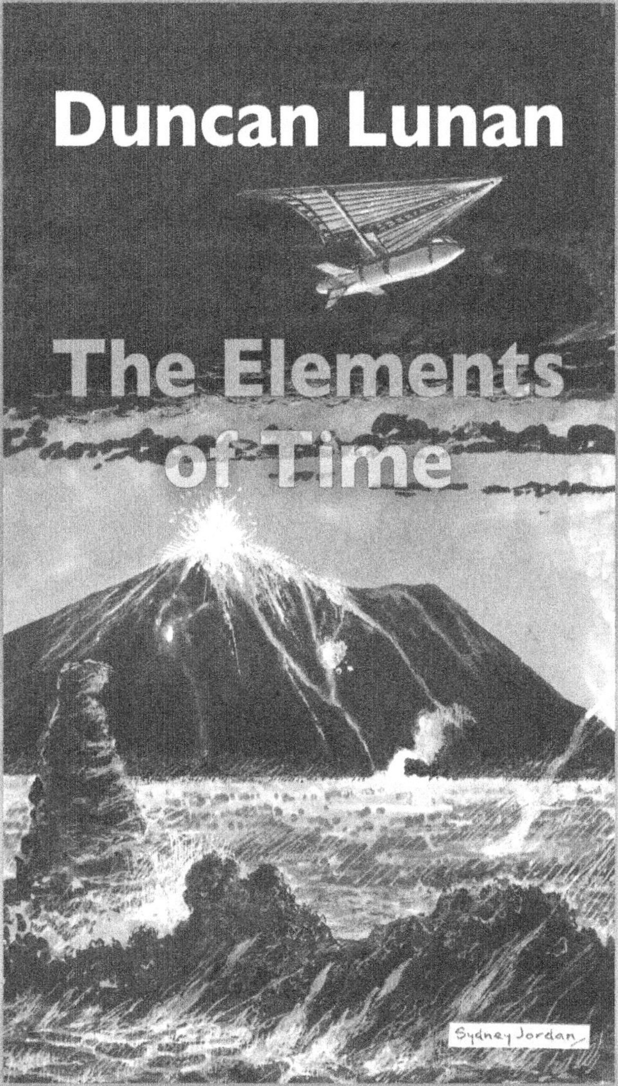
Duncan Lunan
The Elements of Time
Sydney Jordan

Message in a Bottle

Davyne DeSye

This is my 9,346th message to you, whoever you are, wherever you are:

The birds have sung their last. It is with an uncanny certainty that this knowledge settles upon me. For all the living beings that have left me, the loss of these frivolous singing creatures affects me most. Later, when I have the strength of spirit, I will go find a bird, or several, and press their corpses onto the canvas. I want a record of their frail forms that are so fitting to the gauzy insubstantial music with which they once graced my world.

My world. Mine alone. I wonder when you will come back. When you will end the experiment. I expected you long ago.

When I message you next, I will include a miniature of my bird canvas.

Music has always had an animating effect upon me. Music touches me deeply, establishes the strongest connections to my inward self. When we still had working machines that broadcast music, I knew the words, the tunes, the nuances of when to pause, when to allow my voice to roughen, when to push the muscles over my diaphragm to force volume—all the indescribably multitudinous aspects of thousands of songs. Music tuned my energy levels, relaxing me, or riding me to frenzied levels of tension, or pumping me with happy bouncing vigor. I must pause in this message even now, and sing, wondrous that after all these years, melody and words have not left me.

[pause]

I wish there was a way to press a song onto the canvas.

But how to demonstrate the rhythms and melodies and harmonies with just shape and color? I know the rudiments of reading music, whole notes, quarter notes, 4-4 time. Given a keyboard and someone to tell me where middle-C is, I could slowly, excruciatingly, grind out a tune. But to do the reverse, to take a tune and turn it into notes, into the written language of music? That is beyond me. And so, in addition to the music of the birds, I have lost all music.

I have lost all music, other than the music that remains stubbornly within my skull. I cannot paint it, cannot write it, cannot fashion it from my surroundings. To know our songs, you must find me and let me sing them to you. I will not sing into this message. To hear me, you must come to me.

Surely, you are close now.

[pause]

I shall make another sculpture. After I have collected all the birds I can find, after I have pressed their shape into the canvas—I will press them into the sky of my painting, and into the trees because that is where they lived—I will add to my substantial museum a sculpture made up of their bones, and feathers, and sharp hollow beaks. I must design

a way to show the liquid of their eyes because the truth of the lidless sockets will be frightening. You should not be frightened of the birds. They were beautiful.

I will truly be the artist I dream if, in fashioning their eyes, I can do more than merely show liquid orbs, if I can recreate the eager and uneasy meaning they assigned me. The challenge of creating the avian eyes will provide me with purpose.

The sculptures in my museum are not to scale. I tell you this now because I do not believe I have mentioned it in any previous message— although perhaps I have (over these years I forget what I have told you and what I have merely meant to tell). Each sculpture has been crafted with the materials at hand. My bird will be only as big as I can make with all the bird corpses I can find. While the avian population has dwindled in recent months, without the larger predators and scavengers which left me so long ago, perhaps I can recover corpses from months past. If I find only seven or eight, my bird will be small. I hope to find hundreds, even thousands. I wish my bird to rival my squirrel. My squirrel stands loftily above the other sculptures, taller than I am twice again, perched on posterior legs made of hundreds of thousands of posterior legs, balanced on a tail made bushy with individual squirrel tails. I have already told you of my squirrel in an earlier message, but in my pride, I am telling you again. You will be stunned and impressed by my squirrel.

Stephen would have been impressed by my squirrel. And my bird—by the whole menagerie. As our zoologist he was always fascinated by animals. He could talk endlessly of recessive versus dominant traits, subspeciation, mating habits and generational lifespan variations. He did not much like to touch the living creatures he studied—I always had the impression he thought them unclean—but study them he did. That is why I believe Stephen would like my sculptures. They are neither living, nor dirty.

I suppose if I was being true to life they would be a little dirty. I will have to think about that.

[pause]

I miss Stephen. Despite his peculiarities, he loved me well, and was the last to leave me. For the Stephen sculpture, I will save the most beautifully formed, colorful feathers from the birds I collect. I will seek out feathers that have no tears in their vane, and that have the softest, fullest down at the base of the quill. I will search for gentle gradations of color that surpass any genetic necessity of survival. These I will weave into Stephen's hair, or perhaps sew them into the curls of his beard. If I thought I could spare bird skulls or beaks, I would add those to the Stephen sculpture as well. Alas, I must wait and see how many corpses I find.

I will add decorations to the sculptures of Ray and Debra, my parents, as well. Perhaps if I pierce them with one fine long beak each, and save the feathers for Stephen, I can be thrifty with the materials for my sculpture, and quell the whispering that haunts me as a fiend when I feel I have slighted them. Ray and Debra deserve every honor I can give them. Although Stephen undertook to educate me, spent more time with me, and stayed with me the longest, Ray and Debra gave me the physical affection which so repulsed Stephen, and generously shared their allotted portion of food with me. In our limited, enclosed world, their protection of me served no function related to survival of the species. And yet, they protected me. In moments of detached scientific musing, I wonder if their nurturing was merely an instinctual tendency, formulaic and inescapable. I ought, in fairness and because of the unprovable nature of the question, give Ray and Debra the benefit of the doubt. Whatever the motivation, they cared for me.

Despite my desire to achieve an intellectual detachment that is compromised only in my art, the deaths of the other humans have tinctured my mind with a quiet bitterness that creeps upon me when I allow monotony to settle in. It is my sculptures and my canvas that revive me—my creation of something new in a closed environment which theoretically only recycles and recycles and recycles. Through my creations I become divine, and also serve the useful purpose of cataloging, depicting and representing the ruin I have survived. I am sometimes struck with the idea that you have no need of these representations, that you too, on the other side of the barrier, have birds and squirrels, leopards and crocodiles, deer. Our stock came from you. And yet.

[pause]

Enough for today. Tomorrow I will send another message, throw another crumb along the trail toward me. I picture my messages, capsules flowing away from my world, fanning out in the distance, or, perhaps, creating a mountain of messages that avalanches away intermittently. A Doppler line of words that inexorably points to me. I need only wait for the first of them to reach the shores of your awareness.

Except, sometimes I imagine that you are just outside the barrier, receiving my messages, one by one. Reading my thoughts and cataloging concepts. Sometimes I imagine that as I press myself against the cool, reflective barrier— and although I cannot see you—you stand on the other side watching me, studying me as Stephen once studied his animals, enjoying the academic study, but unwilling to touch me.

Are you there?

Are you there?

Davyne DeSye writes from a cozy spot nestled at the base of the Rocky Mountains in beautiful Colorado, USA. She is an author of science fiction, fantasy, horror and romance stories. Her latest novel, *Carapace*, is due for release in June 2017. For more information, visit her website at www.davyne.com.

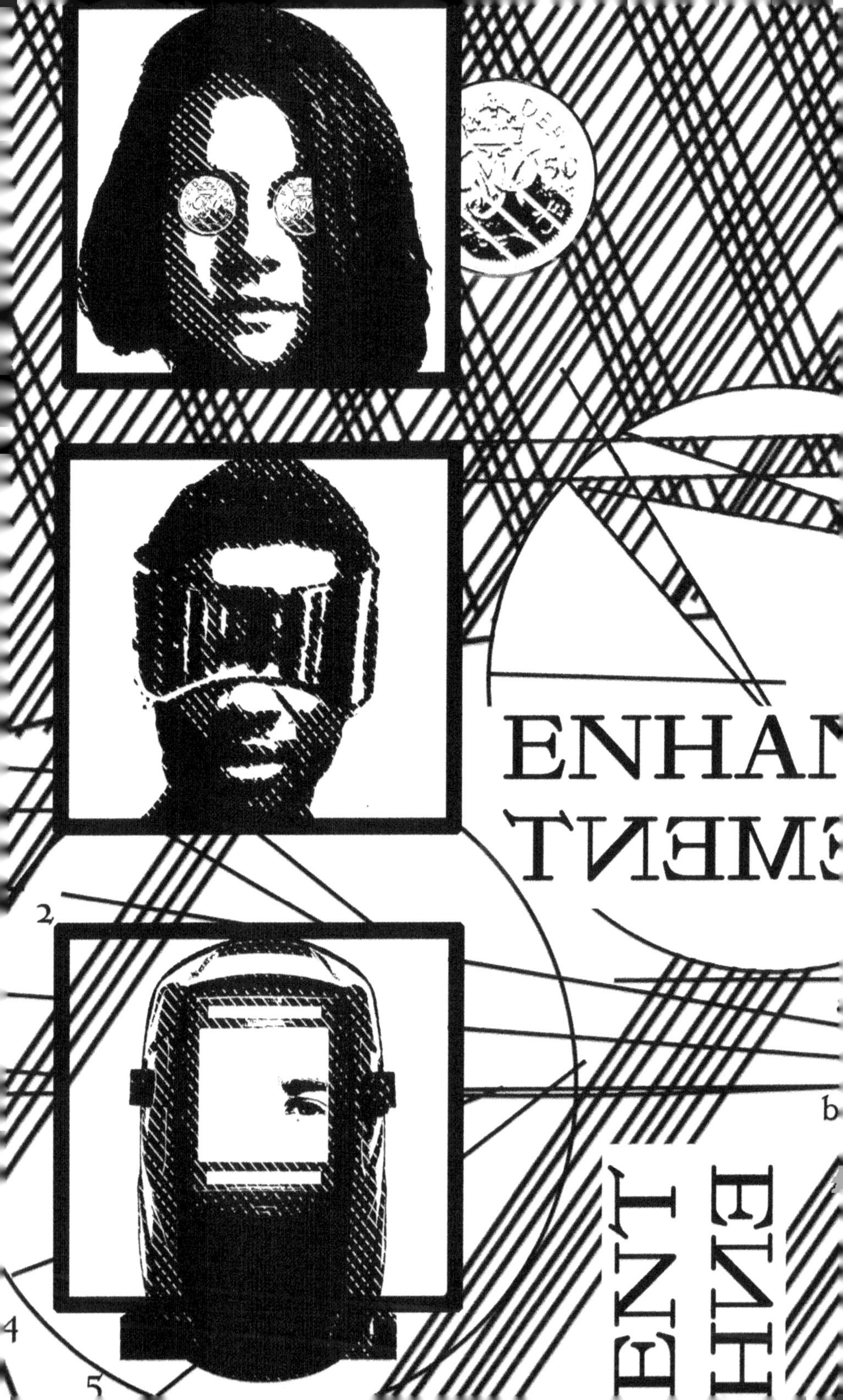
ENHAN
2
4
5

Anyone Can Ask About Enhancement

Terry Jackman

Art: Jackie Duckworth

They'd got to cuddling when Vita mentioned it, then frowned as if she wished she hadn't. Pol laughed. "For Enhancement? Are you kidding? Me? You seen those people?"

The question was rhetorical of course cos everyone had *seen* Enhanced, if only at a distance. Never for long. They came, they did whatever weird thing they'd come for, always wearing darkened visors that disguised their thoughts and feelings, then they disappeared. Pol had never got too near but those who had—who'd talk about it—said they felt repulsed. Enhanced were an exclusive echelon within the Company. They left a chill behind them, and they altered people's lives. And maybe they weren't even human any longer?

That thought stopped his laughter. "They act like they're our gods."

"Why shouldn't they?" She pushed away. "They get the best, a special section of the city, credit ratings we can't even dream of, leave to travel." Vita dropped her voice. "I heard they've even left the planet."

"Yeah? You know a lot about them suddenly."

"You hear stuff, in reception. And I read about it once." Her tone was airy but her face looked… furtive?

His attention sharpened. "You applied!"

Oh, she denied it, several times, but when she left it was without a smile. Sadly he acknowledged it was often like that these days; she came in all warm and eager, but afterwards… she looked around as if she wondered why she'd come. She didn't ask him up to her place any longer either.

His place wasn't so bad, was it? Small, but neat; a bed just long enough to take his length, the usual wall for storage then the counter and the shower. Basic room allowance, but he kept it clean and tidy.

Now he'd better wash away the scent of sex before he went on-shift this evening.

Two long strides and he was in the shower. Pitted plascreen sealed in the mist of the recycled spray which once again was running tepid and uncertain. Twice this week supply had faltered. Ah well, they'd deal with it, when they chose to. He was pretty lucky really, rating a rare single unit in this good multilevel instead of rowdy quarters in a concentrated singles' sector. Stepping out again he measured his 'apartment', seeing it as she might, the bare simplicity and basic fittings. Still half dressed, he sat down on the bed and faced the facts.

It wasn't bad, but it would never be enough for Vita. She already rated half the area again than he did, being an ancillary where he was still a Tasker. Soon she'd pout and say they had no future, look for someone higher up the ladder.

A despairing voice inside his head protested, "But we're good together, and it's not one-sided, she keeps coming back."

"But she won't live with you." The second, sneering voice poured acid. "Not in any Tasker allocation. For Vita it'll be Exec or nothing." And he couldn't give her that, the pay, the perks, the status; didn't matter if he took more risks or laboured extra shifts. Unless…

Her perfume lingered on the sheets. He breathed in deep and stared up at the sterile metal ceiling, heard the sighing in the air vents. She was all he'd ever wanted. He could live without more status, or possessions, but she seemed to need them. She felt… cheated. "She loves me, really, but she can't accept I'm nothing special."

Special. Like. Enhancement.

The words expanded, filling all his senses. Pol pushed it away, revolted, then he slowly drew it back and faced it. Unlikely as it was, it was the only answer to his problem. The Enhanced got good apartments, privileges, status; everything she wanted.

Arguing against his fear he told himself, "You'd work less hours, no more shifts and rotas. You'd live easy, if they took you. And you'd still be you. You've never been a snob, or bad to people, and Enhancement couldn't *force* a person to be antisocial. Hell, your

45

neighbours always have been. You just hear about the worst, that's all, cos face it you don't travel in their circles. Exec down to Tasker, people are still people."

In the coming weeks he reached some tentative conclusions. At his level most of what was 'known' about Enhancement was mere rumour, not to be relied on. But there was a slogan. "Anyone can ask" the Company advised repeatedly on all the public walkways— but they didn't even air recruitment programmes in the Tasker levels. The only thing he knew for sure was folk like him were first in line to be 'dispensed with' as the company described it.

A friend of his had been dispensed with. Pol still saw him sometimes. He didn't want to end up on subsistence, cleaning washrooms, growing dull and vacant. Yet one error by some tired tech was all it took. The risk was always there and he was only 'viable' as long as he was tagged as healthy.

Backward and forward; good and bad; he'd settled nothing, scared of losing her but still unable to persuade himself to a decision. Till the line inspection.

No one knew that it was coming; the foremen hadn't pushed them to work faster, or look more efficient. No one knew except maybe Execs up in their towers. But the shielded window up above them lifted slowly, with a muted whisper almost hidden by the hum of autos and the rattle of the loadlines. It was mid-shift, everyone was busy, but there was a moment's silence he could almost taste between the rows of macro-units. Then each man and woman bent assiduously, faking blindness.

Enhanced. Not one but two. They stayed some time. Pol saw them up there looking, asking questions. When they finally began to turn away the people round him breathed much freer. Only Pol stood rigid.

He'd forgotten to keep his head down, half the line away from where they'd loomed, his wits gone begging, staring upward. Even at that distance one of them had noticed it. A glossy head swung back to face him, mirrored visor baleful. Then the man raised one gloved hand, and slowly raised his visor, and as if compelled Pol pulled away his shielded helmet. Cool, black eyes met Pol's wide blue ones. Time, existence, stumbled. Then recovered.

Nothing actually happened. The Enhanced replaced his visor, backing from the window. Once they left there was a buzz of talk, but Pol stood silent. When a neighbour spoke to him he jerked, looked blankly at the other man then stepped away and left his station, stripping off his dense protective suiting. "Feeling sick," he told the foreman. It was half true.

After a sleepless night he dressed with care in the best of his Tasker issue then, six hours before his shift was due to start, he rode the ramps and walkways to the Company's headquarters. Two long hours of unfamiliar travel, questions, disapproving glances, while the spring inside him coiled tighter. There, a gate guard raised his eyebrows. Entering Execs looked curiously sideways and he felt too big, too clumsy. Still, tight-lipped, he moved to enter.

"You got a pass?" The guard looked unbelieving.

"I heard anyone could ask, about Enhancement."

"Yeah?" The brows rose higher. "Well, that's what they tell me. This'll lead the way. But don't stray, boy, or you'll be arrested." The guard stood back and watched him fumble with the unfamiliar handset. When he finally stepped through an Exec with a senior rating patch called, "Morning, Joff," in passing then, as loudly, "What's *he* doing here?" The door guard muttered something. "What, a Tasker?" Stifled laughter, light and careless. "No chance."

Pol flushed red at the appalling breach of manners but he didn't dare protest, his feelings weren't important here. He went the way this finder took him, yellow if he got it right and red if he went wrong. Commanded by a colour.

ENHANCEMENT

The word was etched across the arch, he'd almost walked right under it, his eyes down on the finder. Now he looked around he faltered. Everything in here was hushed; discreetly lit and coolly spotless, a melange of pale textures. This entrance could have held a hundred folk like him, the glassy floor a lake to drown them. There was no guard this time, no barrier to stop him but it took him several deep breaths to find his courage, scared each breath might smear a shining surface. When he walked, his feet sent muffled ripples of sound around and outward. Ghosts of echoes eavesdropped when he faced the callscreen and his throat constricted.

"Welcome. Please state the reason for your visit."

He'd almost blurted Vita, they'd have thought him crazy. "Er, I came to ask about Enhancement?"

"Are you considering application?"

"Well, I might be." He should still be cautious.

"Please follow the amber line to an interview unit." A thin stripe, glowing orange, surfaced in the floor behind him. No, it definitely hadn't been there when he'd walked across it. Squaring line-built shoulders he marched down it, sinking deeper.

Inside the small white cubicle another disembodied voice took over. "Welcome. Please sit down and face the console." Pol settled gingerly, eyes on the screen before him which became a live mosaic, more subtle colours, somehow reassuring. Or maybe, now he'd got this far the worst was over and his nerves had settled?

"Please sit back. The couch will adjust to your build and posture." Consciously relaxing his bunched muscles, Pol followed the direction, trying to feel calmer. He had made the first decision. Sink or swim, he had gone this far.

"Thank you. The couch is programmed to handle all readings. If at any time these indicate you are unable or unwilling to continue this unit will terminate proceedings. This is a safety feature for your protection. Are you ready to commence?"

"Yes!" He'd gripped the arms then let go quickly, fearing it would tell against him, and he should have spoken softer. But the light dimmed and the cubicle had somehow managed to become a distant, insubstantial haze around him. Nothing but this couch felt solid. The voice sounded female. Dammit, don't get sidetracked.

"Recording now. It will help this unit if you can relax more. Interview commencing." Even before 'she' finished he felt a hundred ghostly touches. From the padded headrest tendrils wrapped across his neck and forehead, clinging on like cobwebs. Tiny silver filaments extended round his wrists and then there was a sudden, stabbing pain between his shoulder blades, though it was gone in seconds.

"Please do not be alarmed, small samples of blood and bone marrow have been taken. At the same time this unit has introduced a minute dose of an enhancing agent into your bloodstream. This may facilitate your own performance and at the same time measure your body's ability to assimilate more treatments."

Pol stared at the flowing shapes that shifted as the voice. He didn't feel any different. Then he did. The outer layer of skin that held him suddenly felt dry and crusted, like the planet's storm-blown surface. His perception tilted. Tremors, earthquakes, spread across his body. Super nova flared inside him, ice caps melted and a tidal wave of violent reaction drowned him.

The unit stayed silent until his breathing steadied then said cheerfully, "As required by law, all relevant information has or will be offered. Your initial reaction is favourable and does not bar you from proceeding. Do you wish to continue?"

Pol's eyes felt wide, the air he breathed felt thinner. But he nodded.

"This unit has registered an affirmative gesture. Before your application begins you must also affirm your willingness to comply with directives on secured information."

"What?"

"This unit is programmed to supply data on the Enhancement process, its history, development and current status; also to enumerate the benefits, or otherwise, of following said treatments. In order to safeguard this confidential data." Here the voice slowed down a fraction. "This unit must be empowered, should your application ultimately fail, for whatever reason, to delete that portion of your memory retaining confidential data."

Pol leaned forward. "Can you do that?"

"I am so programmed."

"Is that legal?"

"Providing you affirm willingness." Pause. "Failure to do so will terminate this interview."

Another silence. Pol watched the screen, but nothing happened. No, of course not. He drew a breath, sat back again and spoke. "OK, I affirm my willingness to comply with your conditions. Will that do it?"

"Thank you. We may proceed."

Like a child Pol immersed himself in story. He discovered that Enhancement went back decades, from its slow and tentative beginnings through a host of evolutions with inevitably some traumatic failures. Sarvij, its original inventor, was among the failures. The unit showed Pol holos of before and after, detailing procedures that destroyed the very man who had believed in their creation. The unit-voice remained aloof, the pictures not so. Pol's heart ached for the man's incurable condition. Why, a touch, a sound, a breath of moving air could cause him torment, despite all attempts at shielding, soundproofed quarters, drugs or padded clothing. Death had truly been the kindest answer.

Eventually the unit murmured, "You are under stress. Please drink." A beaker rose, half full of yellow liquid. Pol didn't query what it was, he simply grabbed and drained it all, and felt his tension lessen. Then he sat a while, head bowed, and thought of those who hadn't made it. Then he sighed and straightened up. At once the unit said, "As required you have now been afforded all relevant arguments. Current procedures, as you have seen, are much safer but there remains some risk. Total rejection currently measures four point four six percent while total assimilation is three point two six percent, with responses between graded as explained. Will you affirm you understood this?"

"Yes, I do," Pol answered grimly.

"Do you still wish to continue?"

Despite the relaxant—or because of it?—Pol's mouth was still dry. "If it goes wrong, the Company takes care of me?"

"The Company undertakes all responsibility for the care and welfare of deserving cases."

He didn't ask for details, not after the holos. "Then… let's get this over."

Questions fired at him out of nowhere: reasoning and problem solving, memories, impressions, ethics, it became a stream of challenges that grew more complex, jolting his imagination. But he felt a rush of satisfaction as his brain ballooned to meet the challenge. He could cope with this! He'd been afraid his lack of book-learning would make him fail but this test didn't ask for textbook knowledge, past the very basics, seemed to him to slide around that aspect.

The unit called a halt and food was offered; did he need it. He felt out of breath as if he had been running, couldn't settle. Trying to be calm he asked, "What time is it?"

"The time is fourteen thirty-seven."

He stiffened. "I should be at work. They'll penalise me for it."

"That has been dealt with, without disclosure of your presence here. Once you initiated the test your foreman was automatically informed you had been transferred to another factory."

In case he failed. Then no one, even him, would ever know what happened? Life would go right on as if he'd never… but he didn't want that any more, for all the doubts he'd come with. Now a magic door had opened, just a crack, but he had glimpsed another state of mind, another world, beyond it.

Yet more questions followed, often abstract and confusing with no clear answers. Pol began to falter but the voice was reassuring. "The interview is almost concluded. It is only necessary to ascertain your current pain threshold. Please stay calm and seated." The shock was gone before he tensed to meet it but it left him wilting. All of this, but would he even rate an offer?

Friends stretched out in his apartment. Bands of real sunlight fractured into rainbow colours as they all raised glasses to their newest Total. Pol smiled back. Three months of treatments; fever, checks and rechecks, hesitations, disbelief. Six months to reach the magic lurking all the time inside him, brighter, keener. Total. One of the three percent. One of the Company's gods!

He had three degrees now, all achieved as practice exercises. He could learn a language in a day and speak it like a native. He could taste the sheer joy of living, every nuance, hear and touch it, like his fellows. He was one of them. They bid him welcome, he could sense their pleasure, and relief that he would join them in their fight to save their people. When they left he sat and looked around at what he had. Here was the status, the material advancement Vita wanted. Smiling at that silly thought he rose and went to show himself to Vita. She'd have worried, now he'd reassure her.

Funny, she hadn't thought about Pol for weeks now, why should a dress she'd never liked remind her? When he'd been transferred so suddenly she'd called at first, left messages, been angry, then she'd grown accustomed to his absence. But she'd missed him, more than she'd imagined. That had rather shocked her. So he wasn't Upper level, he'd been strong and handsome, loving and unselfish, things she hadn't valued till she couldn't find them. When the door chime sounded she got up to answer, unsuspecting, then stepped back. A male Enhanced stood at her door. What had she done? But then the man said, "Vita?" and his hand rose as he tucked the darkened visor in a pocket.

"Pol?" She swayed, then beamed. "It's you? It's really you? You look so…" Then her voice trailed off, for Pol, her doting Pol, was backing from her, face gone rigid.

Terry Jackman (Mrs) is a mild mannered lady living in a quiet village in northwest England. After ten years selling nonfiction her first novel, titled **Ashamet**, is earning five4 star reviews—but she still wonders how her neighbours will react if they find out!
www.terryjackman.co.uk

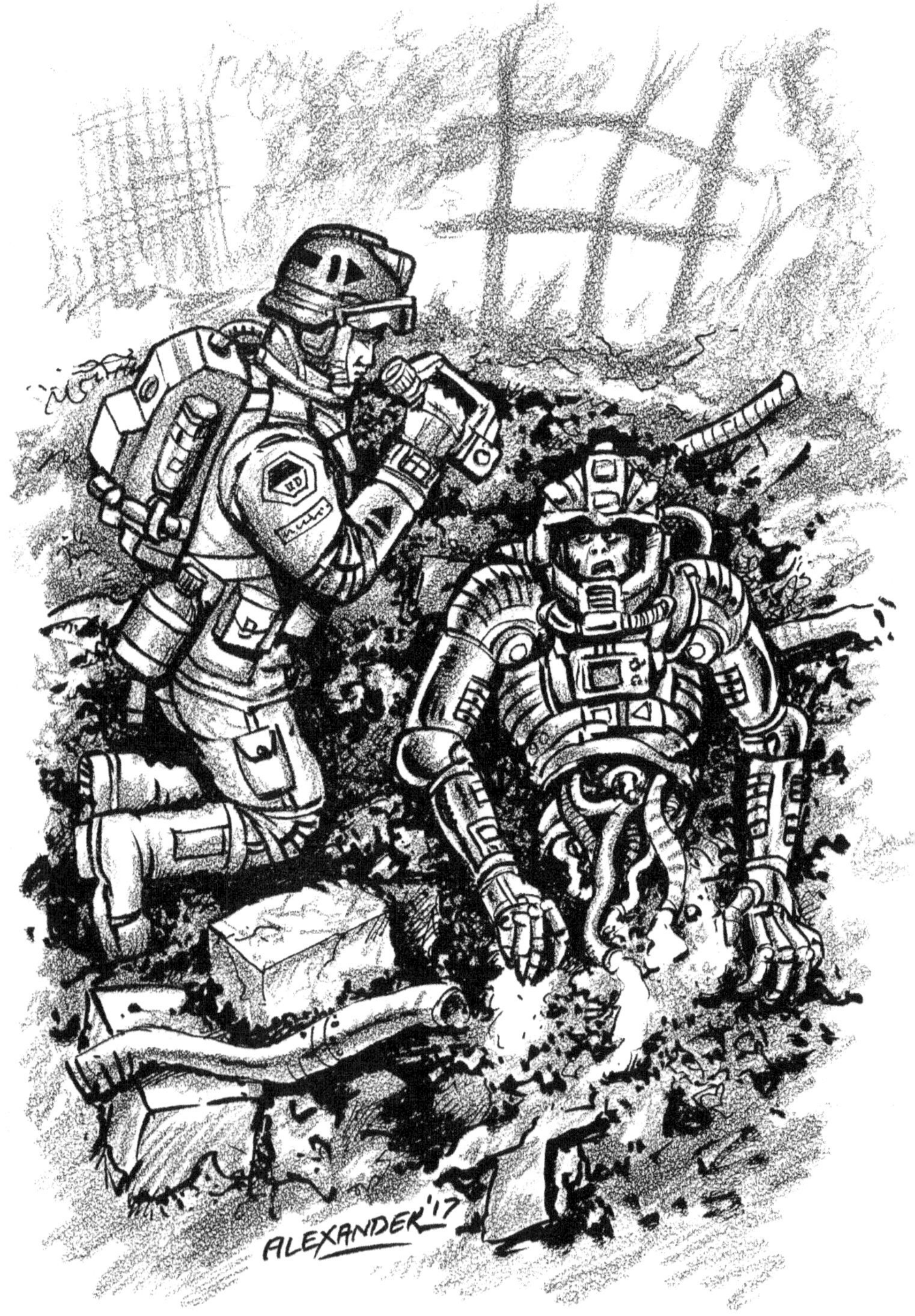
ALEXANDER '17

3.8 Missions

Katie Gray

Art: Dave Alexander

The wind screamed in and out the remains of buildings. It tugged at his clothes, whistled through the holes punched in his helmet for the strap, rattled his ear drums. There'd be a lull in the fighting, if he'd timed this right, but he could hear cracks of missiles in the distance. And there were mines, and sizzling pools left by chemical weapons, and the iSoldiers.

He skittered down a rubbly slope and checked his scope. The signal was a blip and fading. Lock on. Point two clicks, north-north-east. His scope fritzed and he shook it, cursing. The static cleared. He looked up.

The iSoldier was standing over him, a towering figure silhouetted against the burnt-orange smog. The flickering light from a nearby fire danced in its armour, black and gold. He couldn't tell if it was one of theirs. It was armed. Wrist gun. If he bolted it would shoot him dead.

Procedure. He rooted his feet to the ground and held up his wrist to show off his insignia. "Identify."

Like a panther, the iSoldier leapt from the wall. *Snap*. Its wrist-gun retracted. Reaching out, he touched its chestplate. "Identify."

A buzzing. "*Niner-niner-triple-three-delta.*"

"Right," he said, almost relaxing. "As you were."

Its hand shot out, grabbing his vest, knocking all the air out of his lungs. He cried out, gabbling nonsense like, "Friend!" and "On your side!" and "Reds, see? Reds!"

It tugged aside the strap of his vest to get a visual reading of his rank insignia. *Private Carter, Tracey. F-Tech.*

Thump. He dropped to the ground like a discarded sack. In a single leap, the iSoldier bounded over the wall.

"Wanker," Tracey said aloud. It didn't make him feel any better. He adjusted the straps of his vest and levered himself upright.

He checked his scope. Point two klicks. Signal still fuzzy.

He ducked between barbed wire and broken masonry into the chewed-up remains of what had been a car park. He crouched, scanning the open space.

There. A pair of metallic legs spilling out from behind the skeleton of a car. He picked his way over, staying low, and stared at what was left of the iSoldier he'd been sent to patch up.

The legs—just the legs, and a spray of still-hissing fluid. For a happy moment he thought that was all that was left, that the rest of the iSoldier was being ground to dust in the belly of a Beast.

But maybe ten metres further he saw the arms and torso, wires and nerve-enhancements spilling out like tentacles. It was like a broken toy, a rag doll torn in half and left in the dirt.

"Well," he said, "That's going to take some fixing."

Crouching to inspect the legs, he saw the tail end of the spinal cord, white bones visible within the dense circuitry. The only thing left to do was call salvage.

His scope clicked. *Signal online*. He spat a curse. Now he had to check its neural functioning.

The torso was motionless, ragged, but procedure was procedure. He crawled to it. "Identify."

No response. He put his hand on its chestplate.

"Identify, soldier."

Nothing. Sometimes skin contact helped, when the sensors weren't at optimum. He stripped off his glove, but jerked back. The armour was searing hot.

Groping at his belt, he unhooked his probe and forced the helmet open. The face beneath was pale and screwed up, the sound of its panting high and dull in the murky air.

"Identify! Hey!" He patted at the side of its skull. "Status report."

Its eyes opened. "What?" Its voice was an echo of itself, electronics and human vocal cords.

"Identify."

"I don't understand." The electronic voice was flat. The human voice was thick with pain.

Tracey should have realised, then, what had happened. "Identify yourself." Nothing. He detached his scope and held it over the iSoldier's eye, trying for a retinal scan. "Hold still."

976-555- λ.

Oh, no. Jesus, Mary, Joseph and all the Saints in heaven, no. He closed his eyes, swallowed, his throat clasping, dry. It didn't matter, it couldn't matter. The iSoldier didn't even remember.

"I can't feel my legs." Tracey looked down at it hazily, thinking the status report command had kicked in at last and wondering why it wasn't following procedure. "Why can't I feel my legs?"

One last time. "Identify."

"What?" The iSoldier made a noise like it was trying to clear its throat. It was confused by the crackly echo.

"Who are you? What's your name?"

"Private McCray. Eight-oh-oh-niner-fifty."

Tracy almost threw up. Right there, on top of the iSoldier. This couldn't be real. His brain was helpfully scrolling through all the reasons why this shouldn't be possible, all the safeguards in place to ensure iSoldiers never did this, ever.

"Why can't I," said the iSoldier, "What –" It shuddered, and screamed—half staticky roar of electronics, half animal pain.

Tracey covered his ears.

He'd scrapped iSoldiers before. He ought to call salvage, the iSoldier was a tattered mess of fractured spine and chewed-up neural circuits. All he had to do was make the call.

The ever-present rumbling was growing louder. As he dithered, the iSoldier's static-riddled cries were drowned out by the *screeeeech* of bladed wheels chewing through concrete.

"Oh, God!"

The Beast loomed, a misty, disjointed shadow in the fog. He could hear its jaws clashing.

"Oh, Jesus Christ."

Was it Red or Blue? It didn't matter. It didn't care, he didn't care. He was on his feet, ready to run like hell for base, when hot metal closed around his ankle. The iSoldier's hand. It couldn't have seen the Beast, but could hear it, feel it shaking the ground.

"Don't leave me here, you can't leave me here–"

"You're *scrap iron!*" He didn't know if the iSoldier heard him over the pulsing roar of oncoming blades but its brown eyes stared up at him, jerking back and forth in their sockets, alive.

It was the eyes that did it.

Tracey heaved the iSoldier across the tarmac, towards the wreck of the nearest building. It was dead weight, so hot he could feel the heat radiating through his gloves. It was screaming. He thought it was screaming at the Beast but it was screaming at itself. He'd lifted its shoulders and it was looking down at its body, looking at the mass of cables trailing from its severed abdomen, at the void where its legs had been, and its chest plate was vibrating with its screams.

The Beast was almost on them, churning a path through the city, flames and smoke belching out of its grilled mouth. It ate. It gorged itself on rubble and concrete and steel and toxic goo. Tightening his grip, Tracey staggered fast as he could for shelter.

The ground rocked, cracks opened up in the hellish force of its approach, and he fell.

He tumbled down a rubbly slope into the black emptiness that had once been the basement. Gravel and dust fell around him and he curled in on himself, covering his airways. The stink of the fumes, the agonising roar in his lungs, the heat, the dampness of the concrete, the *noise*. It was so loud it wasn't even sound, it was pure, vile sensation pounding at his eardrums, incessant.

When it quieted, he found with dull surprise that he was still alive. He took deep breaths, sobbing in relief, coughing up mouthfuls of dust. He opened his eyes. The Beast hadn't crushed the wall completely. Here and there shafts of sunlight branched through. He might be able to dig himself out.

He heard the iSoldier, still screaming at the top of its lungs. Tracey checked his scope. It was flickery, but functional. Two Red blips, Blues all around them. iSoldiers from the belly of the Beast. If they'd picked up Tracey's signal they'd have come for him already. Sooner or later they'd hear the noise.

He dragged himself over to the iSoldier, wincing as the concrete scraping his raw knees. "Shut up," he gritted out. "Shut up, shut up, *shut up*." He banged on its armour. "You need to be quiet! They'll hear you!"

"Oh, God," said the iSoldier. "Fuck, *fuck*, my legs, where are my *legs*?" It made choked gulping sounds, forcing air back into its failing lungs.

"Will you *shut up*?"

It said, "I can't," and, "Sorry," and, "Hurts." Tracey clawed at the back of its neck, holding his probe between his teeth as he tried to find the right spot to—*yes*—open it up, exposing the cluster of wires at the top of its spine. "What are you doing?"

The wires were half-fused, a tangled mess of still-cooling slag. There was only one thing to do.

"I'm sorry." He jammed in his probe, right up against the first joint of its spine. "This'll only hurt a lot." He thumbed the button.

It screamed, a jagged wail of electronics, arms flexing madly. Somewhere in the mass of trailing cables below its waist something sparked.

And it was done, and the iSoldier was gasping, harsh mechanical sobs falling from its lips. Heat pulsed off its shell. "Oh, God. What did you do to me?"

"I'm sorry," said Tracey lamely. "I needed you to be quiet."

"I can't—it doesn't hurt any more. What did you do?" It flexed its fingers. "I can't feel anything."

"I fried your nervous system," said Tracey. "Needed you to shut up. You were going to get us caught."

The iSoldier's eyes rolled to look at him. "You look familiar."

60

"One of those faces."

It blinked, sucking in air noisily.

Tracey looked up at the tattered shell of the building, hoping that it would die now and let him be.

"Where are my legs?"

It was such a silly question, *where are my legs*, like he'd just forgotten where he'd put them, and Tracey nearly laughed. "I don't know. They were outside, but that Beast probably crushed them."

It digested that. "What happened to me?"

"I don't know. You were in bits when I arrived."

"No, before that."

Tracey shuffled his feet in the dust and grime that coated the floor. He swallowed. His throat was dry. "How much do you remember?"

It wheezed. "I don't know. I was in this—place, I don't know where—they told me I'd been picked out for an experimental treatment, and then I was in a waiting room or—I don't know. It's all in bits. What did they do to me?"

The soft tissues went first. You scooped them out like pumpkins on Hallowe'en. Then the bones. Keep the arm bones and the ribcage and the skull and the spine, but the hip bones and the thigh bones went on the scrap pile, and then—"Oh, God. My *legs*."

Tracey steeled himself. He avoided its eyes. They were the only part of it that looked alive. "If it makes you feel any better, they weren't your original legs."

"Was that supposed to be funny?"

"Not really."

"What happened to my real legs?"

"They weren't used for the procedure. Leg bones—aren't. They don't—I'm sorry."

It was looking at its hands. It mouthed *procedure*.

"This wasn't an experiment, was it? I saw—others. How many people did you –"

61

"I don't know!" said Tracey. "A lot. Thousands. More, maybe. I'm just a field tech, alright? I don't know. They don't tell us anything. They barely even train us."

"They told you more than they told me."

"Shut up," Tracey snapped. "I should have left you out there. I don't know why I bothered saving you."

The iSoldier's eyes blazed . "Oh, you bastard," he said, "You sick, selfish, *fuck* –"

"You are *dead*!"

It went quiet.

"In case you hadn't noticed—you're already dead. Your spine's severed and your entire programming's gotten wiped somehow which means you're undergoing critical neural failure, so I give it maybe two or three hours before your brain disintegrates completely, except you don't *have* two hours. You're overheating. You've got maybe half an hour before what's left of your internal organs cook." He took deep breaths. "So yeah. You're basically dead and I'm basically not and if I'd just *left* you there I might actually have gotten out of this."

Staggering, he sank down on the concrete.

"You could call for help."

"No point. They won't come. They might've if there was enough left of you to save, but there's not, so they won't. They won't come for me. I'm expendable."

The iSoldier wheezed . "You said they didn't train you."

"What?"

"You said they didn't train you. Didn't sound like it just now."

"I was a junior medtech. I got demoted. Happy now?"

There were regulations about executing non-combatants. But there were jobs that needed doing, jobs too dangerous to risk an AI. Field techs, on average, lasted 3.8 missions before their sticky end. It was tidy. It worked, on average.

This was Tracey's fifth mission.

"I woke up on a battlefield without any legs, so no, I'm not happy." A choking sound that was either a laugh or a sob. "What did you do to get demoted?"

"What's it to you? Nothing. I didn't do anything. Piss off." Tracey dn't want to look at it. He didn't want *it* looking at *him*, not with se dancing, living eyes.

u must have done something."

ll, I didn't. It wasn't something I did, it was something I was d to do that I didn't. So I didn't do anything."

quiet for such a long time that he thought it might have urge to look at it grew overwhelming.

nber—a room. It was grey. There were people. Other didn't know what was going on, but something wasn't n something, something –" Its eyes flickered to Tracey's e there."

"

e," it said. "You were there, you said I was to come en you took me into—the other place, and then

snapped, even though it wasn't saying anything. ey made me do it, they ordered me, and when y say—it wasn't my fault." He buried his face ow when I signed up. I swear I didn't know."

e down. You bastard. You doped me. You

lease—just leave me alone. I saved your

tly, wretched sound.

t the smooth metal joints, and it was much of me is left?"

t his face. "Nervous system. Some s, some muscle tissue. Not much dure." Human nervous system, r a better soldier?

"This wasn't an experiment, was it? You knew what you were doing. This is—we were supposed to be the good guys. Aren't we the good guys?"

"I don't know any more. I don't know if we developed this or if we sneaked the technology from them. I'm not sure anyone even remembers."

"How long has it been? Is this the same war?"

Tracey choked out a grim laugh. "Oh, yeah. It's the same wa[r] alright. It never ends. It's been three years since—almost four. [I] remember 'cause..."

" 'cause what?"

"Because you were the first one I worked on." He breathed out. "I remember you. You were blond. Your teeth were crooke[d] liked you."

"*Did* you?"

"You were—charming." *Charming*, a strange word to be usin[g] a battlefield, it felt all wrong in his mouth. "Bit flirty. I thoug[ht] were fit." He almost smiled—but the memory triggered a w[ave] nausea.

The blood coating his latex gloves, the low whine of the equi[pment] the wet sounds it made as—

"I remember," it said. "You were shy. I like shy."

"I wasn't shy, I was piss-terrified," Tracey said, staring at h[im] "I didn't realise how much it was going to suck. Till I spok[e]" The air tasted of metal and spilt fuel. He could hear th[e] sobbing, a rough, grating sound.

It said, "What's your name?"

"Tracey Carter."

"Tracey's a girl's name."

"Fuck you, I saved your life."

"Tracey," it breathed. "Do me a favour, yeah? Don't tell anyone I cried over this."

He snorted out a laugh. "I don't think I'm going to be telling anyone anything."

"You could call for help." The electronics in its voice were warping.

"I already told you, they won't come for me."

"They might. You should try."

"Why do you even care what happens to me?" said Tracey. "I did this to you. I thought you hated me. You *should* hate me."

"Don't want to die hating you," said the iSoldier. "Don't want to die hating anyone."

It was looking at him. Maybe there were tears in its eyes, or maybe that was the way the light was reflecting. "Private McCray. That was your name?"

"Joseph McCray."

"I outrank you." He rubbed his hands over his eyes, up through his sticky hair. "Alright. Fine." He gave his scope a shake and groped through the functions. "I'm pinging the base. Happy now?"

"Yeah, I guess," said Joseph McCray. His metal hand touched Tracey's knee, trying to comfort. Tracey didn't move, because he didn't know what else to do, and because he kind of wanted comforting, even if was from a broken iSoldier.

The light was dimming. He wasn't sure if night was falling or if it was the thickening smoke. His scope flickered and died for good. He drank half the water he had left and ate his compacted nutrient bars.

He tried to climb out, dragging himself up the slope. He put his weight on a loose clump of brick and skittered all the way down, scraping open

65

his hands and knees. He picked the grit out of his palms and began again.

"You won't make it."

"Oh yeah?" He scrabbled to find footing, staring up at the rays of musty light. Freedom was so close he could taste it.

"It's like—I grew up near this old quarry. There was one side that was too steep to climb. We always tried but we never made it, it was like walking on ice—and one time my mate tried it and he fell and broke—my mate, he –" His growling voice cut out. Tracey lost his tenuous footing, slithering down to the concrete. "My mate, his name was—he was my best mate since forever, I should know his name—why don't I remember his name?"

"I dunno." Tracey dusted off his hands. He gave his scope a shake. Still nothing. He steeled himself. "Your memory centres might be starting to break down."

"No." Joseph waved a metal hand at him. "No, you said that wouldn't happen. You said I'd be dead first."

"Said you'd be dead before your neural circuits went kaput. Never said you'd be dead before you started to—you know. Go."

"Go *where?*" Joseph clutched at the ground, trying to lever himself upright. His fingers gouged tracks through the concrete. "What's going to happen to me?"

"I don't know. I don't know! You've still got most of your brain. I don't know anything about brains. I'm a tech, not a neuroscientist." He climbed. Hand, foot. Hand, foot.

"If you get out –" Joseph's voice was tinged with panic. Perhaps it always had been. The electronic voice box was fading, the iSoldier's voice falling to an unintelligible hum. "If you get out, are you just going to leave me here?"

Hand, foot. Hand, foot.

"I don't want to die like this. Not alone. Don't leave me to die like this alone, *please.*"

His hand met something jagged under the dirt. He dragged himself upwards even as blood smeared on the dust, fuelling his screaming muscles with mind-numbing desperation. He hadn't known he wanted to live this badly.

He fell, tumbling like Jack down the hill. Something jarred in his arm. He cradled it to his chest. "You said yourself. I'm not going to make it."

"Did I?" There was a clicking sound. Tracey almost didn't recognise it as a gulp. "I don't remember."

Tracey rubbed at his face, trying to scrub away the dirt. The palm of his hand stung. His arm throbbed. He wiped his oozing nose on his wrist. He could smell something over the dank, dusty stench of the basement. It smelled like meat cooking. "Do you smell that?"

"Smell what?" said Joseph. "Can't smell anything."

"Yeah." Tracey kept his hand over his nose. "Probably for the best."

"Why? What is it?"

"Nothing." He tested his arm. It bent, but when he reached out a shock of pain jolted up to his shoulder. "I think I'm stuck here."

"You could call for help."

"I already did." He worked his arm, hoping it would get better if he stretched it, but it hurt more and more the more he moved it.

"Right."

Joseph brought a hand up in front of his face, flexing each finger-joint in turn. "Is that my hand?"

"Yeah." Tracey flexed his own fingers. It hurt.

"What happened to me?" said Joseph. "Why am I a robot? I don't—I don't remember what happened to me."

Tracey could hear a hissing, crackling sound coming from somewhere within Joseph's armour. The last of his cooling system giving way. He pressed a hand to his mouth and tried not to retch.

If he could get out—which was unlikely, with a busted arm—maybe, just maybe, he'd get back to base before the Blues got him. And then what? He'd live to die another day, blown into chunks or fried by a nerve-shell.

Or he could die here, cold and alone in what was left of a basement with what was left of an iSoldier.

The sizzling was getting louder.

Joseph let out a yelp. "What?" He was panting, in-out-in-out, rough gasps of air. "What—why can't I –" He was staring at his hand—but he wasn't. His eyes were roaming about in their sockets, unfocused. His optic nerve had severed.

Staggering over, Tracey knelt beside him. "What's wrong?"

"I can't see," Private McCray choked. "Oh God, I can't see."

Tracey took a deep breath. He tried to sound calm. "It's alright, Private. You're fine."

"Why can't I see? I remember—fighting. There was a blast. What happened to my eyes?"

"You got hit," said Tracey. "You'll be okay. I promise. I'm a medtech."

Maybe Joseph believed him, maybe he didn't. "What was it? Nerve shell?"

"Yeah. One of those bastards."

"I can't feel my legs, are they –"

"You're going to be fine. Just need some fixing, that's all." His voice was getting rough. God, he was thirsty. "I called for help, remember? There'll be more medics here any minute now."

"Yeah." Dark fluid seeped out of the corner of Joseph's mouth. "Listen, do me a favour and don't tell Sergeant Reid I cracked up over this."

"Don't worry. I can keep a secret." Tracey clutched his injured arm to his chest. The air around them shimmered. "I'll tell him you were stoic and manly throughout."

Private McCray laughed. He choked. The crackling was getting louder. "What's that noise. Feels like—air bubbles inside my skin."

"It's nothing, don't worry about it." Tracey could feel the heat coming off the armour on his face.

"Sounds like—sounds like steak cooking. Steak cooking. My Dad used to make it on Sundays. Days. Every and chips. Always—well done." He rasped. "Smells good."

"Yeah, yeah I know." Tracey hoped he sounded soothing. "You just relax now, Private. Help's coming."

"Not supposed to relax too much. When you're concussed, you're supposed to stay awake. Awake." A rumbling was building on the edge of Tracey's hearing. "You have to count."

"Count?" The light was going away, as if the sun was setting—or a shadow was looming.

"Between the thunder. Ever been struck by lightning?"

And he was gone. A light went out behind his eyes. Nothing left but the hissing and popping of his innards gently cooking themselves. Tracey prodded at his face, trying to get his eyes to close. He could only get one shut. The other hung open, like he was winking. He used the last of the charge in his probe to force the helmet.

It was just half an iSoldier, leaking steam and fluids onto the filthy concrete.

Tracey backed away. He found his canteen. His fingers shook as he unhooked it from his belt and slowly drank.

He could hear a distant roaring. There was no sense conserving water. He finished it off, guzzling what little was left. It spilled tepid down the front of his vest.

A minute passed in the building haze, fingers slipping on the damp plastic of his canteen, watching motes of brick dust dancing in the last rays of light till they were blotted out for good.

The roar of the Beast was almost upon him. Clawed feet tearing through steel and concrete, churning up the city to feed itself. It had to be just outside, it was so loud, but the noise kept on building, building till it hurt, till the whole world narrowed down to just the *roar* and the hurt.

He screamed into it till his throat was raw. He couldn't hear himself screaming, couldn't hear a thing until it stopped.

It quieted so suddenly he staggered, almost fell. He opened his eyes, squinting in the sudden light, in the dust-cloud than enveloped him. It had cracked open the building. It loomed over him, bigger than anything he'd ever seen. The low thrumming of the engines was distorted, as if he was under water. He unclasped his hands from his ears and found smears of blood in his palms. He hadn't even noticed.

A figure, stark against the light. Another, and another. iSoldiers. On the march.

He heard faint underwater sounds of metal dragging on concrete. They were dragging away what was left of Private McCray to be recycled. Something like hope fluttered in his chest. Maybe they'd come for him after all.

The nearest iSoldier was staring at him through the dusty, warped gloom the world had become. "Identify." His throat was raw, he could barely get the word out. He swallowed, coughed, tried again. "Identify!"

It raised an arm. In its wrist, a blue glow.

The shot was pure, searing agony, every nerve-ending in his body screaming at once, until he was gone, blank, empty –

He came to with cold concrete at his back, and noted with dull surprise that he was still alive. For a split second there was elation, elation at somehow clinging to consciousness despite everything –

The second blast coursed through him like a bucket of cold water. There was pain. There was nothing, a wave of numbness. There was enough time to think, to register that his nervous system was giving out under the strain, the nerve-shell was shutting it down, leaving him numb, and he thought, he thought –

– A *snap* of power. A spasm. A breath.

Tracey opened his eyes and saw white light. He couldn't move. There were wires in him, tiny hooks all over his body, holding him in place. There were people pacing around him.

He was still alive. Or—not *still* alive. Rolling his eyes upwards, chest heaving, he saw the RESC unit still sparking. *Of course*, he thought.

"Help me."

The figures in the room kept moving, kept circling him, like sharks. They were wearing masks over their faces.

Silence.

"Who are you?" There was an insignia on the RESC unit, but though he rolled his eyes up and squinted, he couldn't make out the colour. It looked a sickly purple.

A high-pitched whine. He knew that sound.

"What—no."

Apparatus glided into view, a squat box with blades and serrated wheels and needles, its arms swinging over him, and he knew that apparatus, it was nauseatingly familiar.

"No," he said. "No, you—you don't want me—I'm a medtech, not a soldier." He gulped down air, the sound of the apparatus powering up filling his ears. "Look at me—you don't want me—no, no no no no –"

The glistening point of a needle angled towards him and in the moment before it stabbed down, he saw that the people around him weren't wearing masks. Those were their faces, metallic, expressionless visors, and when he twisted, trying to escape the needle, he saw another helmet, set aside for him.

A pinprick of pain as the needle went in and as the world swam around him, he had time to think *right, of course*. Because there was no sense in fighting this, no sense in worrying about Blues and Reds. They'd already lost. All of them.

Katie Gray is an author of science fiction, fantasy and science-fantasy living and working in Edinburgh. She has a master's in creative writing from the University of Edinburgh and transcribes bank statements to pay the bills. Her work has appeared in *Orbis* and *Freak Circus* and she's currently putting the finishing touches on a fantasy novel.

Quantum Flush

Daniel Soule

Tristram Stumblebawb materialised in a back alley of Alexandria in 47BCE, while Julius Caesar's warships attacked the ancient Egyptian port. Mission parameters were simple: confirm the cause of the great library's destruction; obtain texts unknown; and, above all, don't change the timeline. Oh yeah, and this was his last chance.

If that wasn't hard enough, Tristram was backed-up, as always, because the worst thing about time-travel is the constipation. Tristram had a bit of thing about public conveniences anyway, but displacing to a new time vector made it excruciating. The Sacking of Rome and the Great Fire of London were just the same. Hitler's bunker was a nightmare and don't get him started on the whole 'out of Africa' misadventure. Although, one thing he'd say for the bunker: "Amazing toilets". Nazi high command faced the end with an embarrassment of quilted tissue. And Africa taught him three things: improve his click-languages; up the cardio; and always carry a stash of loo roll, as he did now under his toga.

Recruited straight from Oxford, Tristram was the only linguist on the project. He was an unlikely kaironaut: zero physics, even less engineering, and no survival skills to speak of; but the lad was a walking Babel. It was those linguistic talents that gave him this last chance and Greek of this period was his specialty.

Reconnoitre went well and the costume department had done wonders. Papyrus papers of a visiting scholar were tucked into Tristram's toga, along with a purse of gold for bribes. But even amid the grandeur of the classical world all he could worry about was locating a latrine, because after the constipation came 'the flush', and there was no holding it back.

The physicists had tried to explain, or hypothesize was more accurate: something to do with entanglement, invalidating the information paradox, and particles "settling down," was how they put it, using inverted-comma-fingers. Essentially, they thought after displacement the kaironaut was a little physically "fuzzy" (they used the fingers again) in the new time vector and constipation was symptomatic of this (more fingers) "fuzziness." *Id Est*, they didn't really know.

Implanted lenses recorded the exterior splendour of the library. Archaeologists would pore over the detail when he got back. If he did a good job this time, command might consider him for the Neolithic scoutings. Göbekli Tepe had been on Tristram's wish-list from the start. The prospect of discovering Neolithic languages was tantalizing. And the project had learnt lessons from the 'out of Africa' debacle – saving the timeline and humanity... just.

Taking Tristram's paleness as an indication of higher class, the library's clerk looked over his papers, smiled, and spoke in Greek. Feeling bunged-up and filled with foreboding, the kaironaut was shown to the scrolls. Tristram panned his head for the lenses to record the layout on the way to the reading hall. Traversing the cool marble floor, nine muses looked down. Oil lamps burnt, lighting drafty corners.

The clerk left him to browse. For the first time since displacement the heavy feeling left him. His heart raced. This is what he'd signed up for: forgotten texts and languages. Well, forgotten until the *Surveying History in Time* project.

There were lost works of Greek, Babylonian and Egyptian philosophy, architecture, medicine and astronomy but he'd been ordered to visit mathematics and engineering.

Once displaced, kaironauts have limited time. They record as much as possible, but they have to prioritize. For each scroll he unwedged and rolled out he knew his lenses recorded priceless information, but only fragments.

Wait! There it was... Archimedes' lost work, *On Sphere-Making*, and another not in the records. Tristram must read quickly and move on.

They were like new, rolling out beautifully, skillfully penned. Working through the text, Tristram switched to take a high definition sample. He shifted excitedly from foot to foot. This would rewrite their understanding of the ancient world. Those Neolithic languages were coming closer.

And then it hit: the flush. "Oh Zeus!" The excited hopping wasn't excited anymore. A cold sweat beaded on Tristram's forehead. Without the care it deserved, the skinny kaironaut scooped up *On Sphere-Making*, and scuttled off, buttocks clenched. It was a matter of time; wasn't it always?

"Where is it? Where is it?" He could also be fluently desperate in ancient-Greek.

The sound of Tristram's gurgling bowels alerted a swarthy scholar, perhaps of Babylonian descent, who raised his head from a codex and pointed to an archway.

He was off, fumbling for the loo roll in his robe, juggling the unfurling papyrus scroll and skidding into the lavatory.

"I woke up on a battlefield without any legs, so no, I'm not happy." A choking sound that was either a laugh or a sob. "What did you do to get demoted?"

"What's it to you? Nothing. I didn't do anything. Piss off." Tracey didn't want to look at it. He didn't want *it* looking at *him*, not with those dancing, living eyes.

"You must have done something."

"Well, I didn't. It wasn't something I did, it was something I was supposed to do that I didn't. So I didn't do anything."

It was quiet for such a long time that he thought it might have died. The urge to look at it grew overwhelming.

"I remember—a room. It was grey. There were people. Other soldiers. We didn't know what was going on, but something wasn't right, and then something, something –" Its eyes flickered to Tracey's face. "You were there."

"No I wasn't."

"Yeah you were," it said. "You were there, you said I was to come with you, and then you took me into—the other place, and then you –"

"Shut up!" Tracey snapped, even though it wasn't saying anything. "I didn't want to. They made me do it, they ordered me, and when you don't do what they say—it wasn't my fault." He buried his face in his arm. "I didn't know when I signed up. I swear I didn't know."

"You were holding me down. You bastard. You doped me. You *bastard*."

"Stop it," said Tracey. "Please—just leave me alone. I saved your life, didn't I?"

"Fuck you." It made a ghastly, wretched sound.

It was staring at its hands, at the smooth metal joints, and it was crying, or trying to cry. "How much of me is left?"

"I don't know." He scrubbed at his face. "Nervous system. Some of your skeleton. Heart and lungs, some muscle tissue. Not much soft matter. It's an extensive procedure." Human nervous system, mechanical body. Who could ask for a better soldier?

"This wasn't an experiment, was it? You knew what you were doing. This is—we were supposed to be the good guys. Aren't we the good guys?"

"I don't know any more. I don't know if we developed this or if we sneaked the technology from them. I'm not sure anyone even remembers."

"How long has it been? Is this the same war?"

Tracey choked out a grim laugh. "Oh, yeah. It's the same war alright. It never ends. It's been three years since—almost four. I remember 'cause..."

" 'cause what?"

"Because you were the first one I worked on." He breathed in, out. "I remember you. You were blond. Your teeth were crooked. I liked you."

"*Did* you?"

"You were—charming." *Charming*, a strange word to be using on a battlefield, it felt all wrong in his mouth. "Bit flirty. I thought you were fit." He almost smiled—but the memory triggered a wave of nausea.

The blood coating his latex gloves, the low whine of the equipment, the wet sounds it made as—

"I remember," it said. "You were shy. I like shy."

"I wasn't shy, I was piss-terrified," Tracey said, staring at his knees. "I didn't realise how much it was going to suck. Till I spoke to you." The air tasted of metal and spilt fuel. He could hear the iSoldier sobbing, a rough, grating sound.

It said, "What's your name?"

"Tracey Carter."

"Tracey's a girl's name."

No polished ceramic bowl awaited but at least there was a clean hole over a well-engineered latrine, lit by more lamps. A little drafty though.

The good thing about togas is that they can be hoisted up in a flash. Tristram released the flush, with something between a cry and a sigh. This also meant that it wouldn't be long until he displaced back again. He must hurry.

In his haste, a single, delicate piece of twenty-first century toilet paper, accidently slipped from his grasp. It wafted into the air, suspended like a frog floating in a magnetic field, before the breeze caught it again, propelling it towards a lamp.

Toga hitched up, underwear cuffing his ankles together like the wrists of a guilty man, Tristram pitched forward, fingers outstretched helplessly. His lenses recorded every detail. The tissue grazed the flame; its carbon kindled, dancing inevitably towards *On Sphere-Making*. The papyrus ignited with frightening speed, unrolling as it did towards a neat pile of linen for hand-drying and the inferno was set. Linen caught drapes, drapes caught wood and so on in a chain reaction.

The last thing Tristram Stumblebawb's lenses recorded was his futile flapping at flames as he displaced back into the *Surveying History in Time* project.

At least he'd discovered the cause of the libraries destruction, and technically he hadn't changed the timeline. Two out of three wasn't bad. But, those Neolithic scoutings seemed further away than ever.

Daniel Soule was an academic but the sentences proved too long and the words too obscure. Northern Ireland is where he now lives. But he was born in England and raised in Byron's home town, which the bard hated but Dan does not. They named every other road after Byron. As yet no roads are named after Dan but several children are.

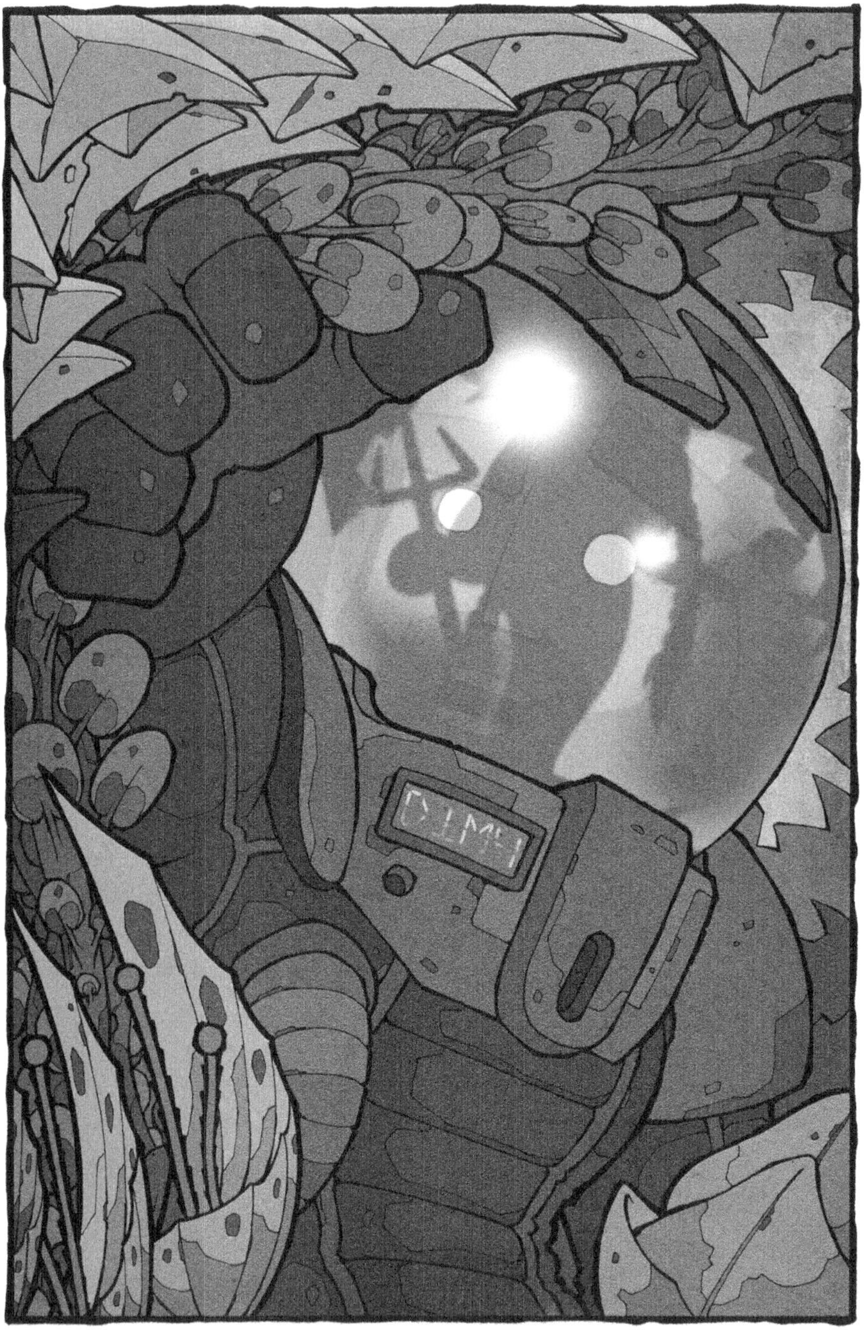

Something Fishy

David L Clements

Art: Stuart Beel

I t was a fish. **Unquestionably**. A large fish, coloured mostly a deep, dark blue, but with large pink spots scattered across its dorsal side. The colours appeared especially vibrant in the light of this planet's bluer, hotter sun.

The fish was standing on its tail—or at least that's how it seemed, since the tail disappeared into the leaf mould on the forest floor— and it was singing.

The song sounded operatic, but Peter wasn't sure. He didn't like opera—he found it too artificial, too pretentious. It was one of the few things he and his now-distant partner Michelle couldn't agree on, but at this point in his mission he'd been away so long he'd even started to miss those disagreements.

A singing fish wasn't what you expected to find on a planetary survey. The unexpected, yes—he remembered stories about the semi-sentient plant-life on one planet, and the time taken to work out that the small, scurrying creatures, with no detectable ways of eating or excreting, were actually self-motile seed pods, not animals after all. Or the planet-wide symbiotic ecosphere, where 'prey' animals volunteered themselves to be eaten by 'predators'. But a giant fish, as tall as a human, in a forest of purple serpentine-trees, ten miles from the nearest large body of water, standing on its tail and singing opera? No, this wasn't right.

He checked that the remotes surveying that area of the forest were functioning. These little robots resembled the local equivalent of birds. Two were perched on the twisting leaves of a tree observing the fish's operatic display. The remote's performance metrics were optimal, the video and audio feeds fully encrypted and suffering no dropouts. He even checked his own implants, making sure they weren't glitching or suffering a malware attack, though the chances of that happening this far beyond the rim of inhabited space were minimal. As far as Peter could tell he was the only human for several light years in every direction, and, since Michelle had checked them out before he had left home, he couldn't have brought anything with him.

Everything looked fine. Short of rebooting the entire system they were the best checks he could do. And yet the fish still stood there singing.

Peter was slower to action, more careful about examining all the options. But for something as unusual as this he missed Michelle's quick-witted insight. He looked wistfully at the image of her that was displayed in the corner of his desktop.

He wasn't far from the singing fish. The flitter could be there within minutes if he pushed it supersonic, but doing that would break protocol. He should head out immediately, in case the piscine operatic performance ended soon. Protocol, in principle, required him to obtain permission before mounting any direct interaction with the planetary environment.

Contamination—of planet or surveyor—carried danger. This had been drilled into Peter during training. The years of survey work since then had shown him that many breakthroughs had come from breaking protocol. The secret of the self-motile seedpods had only been revealed when a frustrated surveyor trod on one by accident.

He had met Michelle during training for the survey corps. She was French, one of the European Union's recruits, while he was from the US. All of them had been eager to explore the frontier, but she and Peter had bonded because they were also fascinated by alien biology. The survey corps' main job was locating targets for colonisation, but it was just as important to catalogue the infinite variety of life in the galaxy, and that's what really motivated Peter and Michelle—finding those planets that should be avoided, those that should be protected, and identifying the few biospheres that could peacefully coexist with Earthly biology.

That was why Peter was out here, on his own because of cuts. He had protested against them the last time he had been home, but to no avail. The cuts, combined with undiminished ambition, meant

the survey corps was spread thin across the myriad planets beyond the frontier.

A message to headquarters about the fish, and a request to make direct intervention, would take days to traverse the galaxy's wormhole network, and longer to make its way through review panels and risk assessment groups.

Peter could make his own decisions in emergencies, or in exceptional circumstances. He'd got to know the biology of this world pretty well. He was currently in the tropics, not that they lived up to that name. He had spent three months in the frigid arctic wastes, which got far colder than the Antarctic but still managed to support some life. The tropics were teeming in comparison.

He'd found that the basic building blocks of life on this planet were similar to a thousand others. Long chain molecules—not DNA but similar—stored genetics, while amino acids, in various configurations, were the building blocks of protein-analogues. The planet was comfortable enough for colonisation—especially, thought Peter, in the tropics—and compatible enough biologically that it would work. You couldn't get much food value from local species, except as indigestible roughage, but nothing was actively poisonous to Earthly biology. Human food crops could be grown and much more besides. On that basis the planet might be slated for a more detailed and a more intrusive examination.

If there was intelligent life here, or something unusual that Peter had yet to spot, then things could be very different. Unusual biology could earn the planet protected status, and if he found any signs of intelligence he'd have to pull out immediately and wait for the first contact team. The singing fish was definitely odd, and might even be a sign of intelligence, and that would certainly make these circumstances exceptional.

If Michelle were in his place she would head out immediately. She kept telling him he was too cautious.

He reviewed the incoming data, sinking into the virtual reality his implants built from the remotes' signals. The fish was still there. It was singing what he thought was an aria.

He had to see it, and hear it, for himself.

Decision made, he rapidly stuffed himself into one of the suits needed for protection from the local biosphere. The suit would also protect the local ecology from the Earthly biosphere Peter carried around and inside himself. Then he walked the short distance from the main monitoring centre of his small habitat to the hanger and the tiny atmospheric flitter that it contained.

The flight took less time than it took to get ready. The autopilot landed the flitter in a clearing conveniently close to the singing fish. A few moments later he looked out onto an alien environment.

At first sight, the forest wasn't unlike those at home. Tall tree-analogues, ground-covering plants, and decaying leaves spread all around. After a few moments the differences began to become apparent. The colours were wrong. The sun in the sky was too blue. The leaves on the trees were a bluey shade of green, their chlorophyll-analogue better adapted to working with the light from their star. The shape of the leaves was different too, not matching any of the basic leaf-forms you would find on Earth or the colonised planets, with leaf-substems spiralling upwards towards the light. All of this, and much more, was the result of a separate evolution that derived nothing from the basic assumptions of Earthly biology that were hard wired in every species on Earth for the last three and a half billion years.

Peter paused as he made his way out of the airlock, glancing at the array of self-defence equipment stored there.

The biology of this planet was not without its hazards. There were apex predators in all the environments he had studied. The largest he was aware of were the ursinoids that roamed these equatorial forests. His remotes had found no trace of ursinoid activity anywhere near the singing fish so he was probably safe from them, but it was the potential unknown aspects of this biosphere that gave him pause for thought. Predators didn't always work in obvious ways. He remembered a planet where the females of the dominant herbivore species were lured to their deaths by a predator that almost perfectly mimicked the mating displays of the males. The unfortunate females would be seduced into a cave they thought had been prepared as a nesting site by the male only to be devoured by the much larger sedentary predator that lurked there.

It might be that the singing fish was the mating display of an unknown large animal, or the lure of an even larger predator. Caution was called for, but he couldn't blithely mow down members of potentially unique species using some of the more destructive devices that lay before him.

After a few moments thought he selected one of the non-lethal weapons—a combined net and adhesive spray gun that was capable of immobilising any creature smaller than a mammoth. Then, after a few moments further thought, he also selected a diamond-edged machete. He wasn't planning to use this as a weapon, though. It would be an excellent escape device if he stuck himself in his own netting since gluing yourself to a tree on an alien planet, light years from the nearest assistance could be fatal as well as embarrassing.

With the weapons strapped to his belt Peter stepped out of the airlock. He took a few moments to get his bearings, then headed to where he hoped the fish was still singing.

He heard it before he saw it. The fish's voice ranged from a deep, profound bass to the clear crystal tones of the best soprano. He paused to listen before he stepped into the clearing to see the fish for himself. There were hints of polyphony to the singing and, despite his usual attitude to opera, he was beginning to find its tones fascinating, almost enjoyable.

He didn't rush in. The fish continued to sing with no sign that it was going to stop any time soon. He circled the clearing, using the scanners in his suit linked to those in the remotes that watched from above. Terahertz radar in the remotes probed the ground around the fish, looking for any evidence that it was a part of some larger, nastier predator. Seismometers embedded in the boots of his suit used his footsteps to probe the ground in search of burrowing or pre-existing tunnels, while vents in his helmet sifted the atmosphere for any chemicals that might act as pheromones or poisons for local species.

They all found nothing. Peter reviewed the results on the headup display in his helmet and came to a conclusion. It was safe.

He moved into the clearing, seeing the fish clearly with his own eyes for the first time.

Its voice rose to a crescendo, the song reaching a dramatic climax just as he arrived, a conclusion worthy, as far as Peter could tell, of the best operas and best opera singers in the world.

The song stopped. The fish turned towards Peter, bowed, and disappeared.

He smiled, feeling a fool. He should have guessed it at once. The signals from the remotes were secure, but Michelle had checked his

implants six months ago, the day he had left for this survey, and must have installed code that would put on this show for him.

She loved opera almost as much as she loved him—maybe more. But most of all she loved a good joke.

A window appeared in his field of view, showing her smiling face.

"I hope you don't mind too much! I had so much fun planning this and I think you might have enjoyed the music. Now it's only three more months until we are together again!"

His smile broadened. "Why a fish?" he asked as the recorded message paused, almost as if Michelle had expected him to ask a question.

"I really couldn't resist the idea when I worked out where you would be today. Happy *poisson d'Avril mon chére*!"

David L Clements is an astrophysicist at Imperial College London, where he mostly works on extragalactic astronomy and observational cosmology. His science fiction has been published in *Analog, Clarkesworld* and Nature (as have some of his scientific results) as well as numerous anthologies. His first story collection, *Disturbed Universes,* was published by NewCon Press in 2016. He has also written a non-fiction book, *Infrared Astronomy: Seeing the Heat*, published by CRC Press. Despite a developing interest in bioastronomy, he has yet to find life on any worlds other then Earth, but he's working on it!

The Beachcomber

Mark Toner

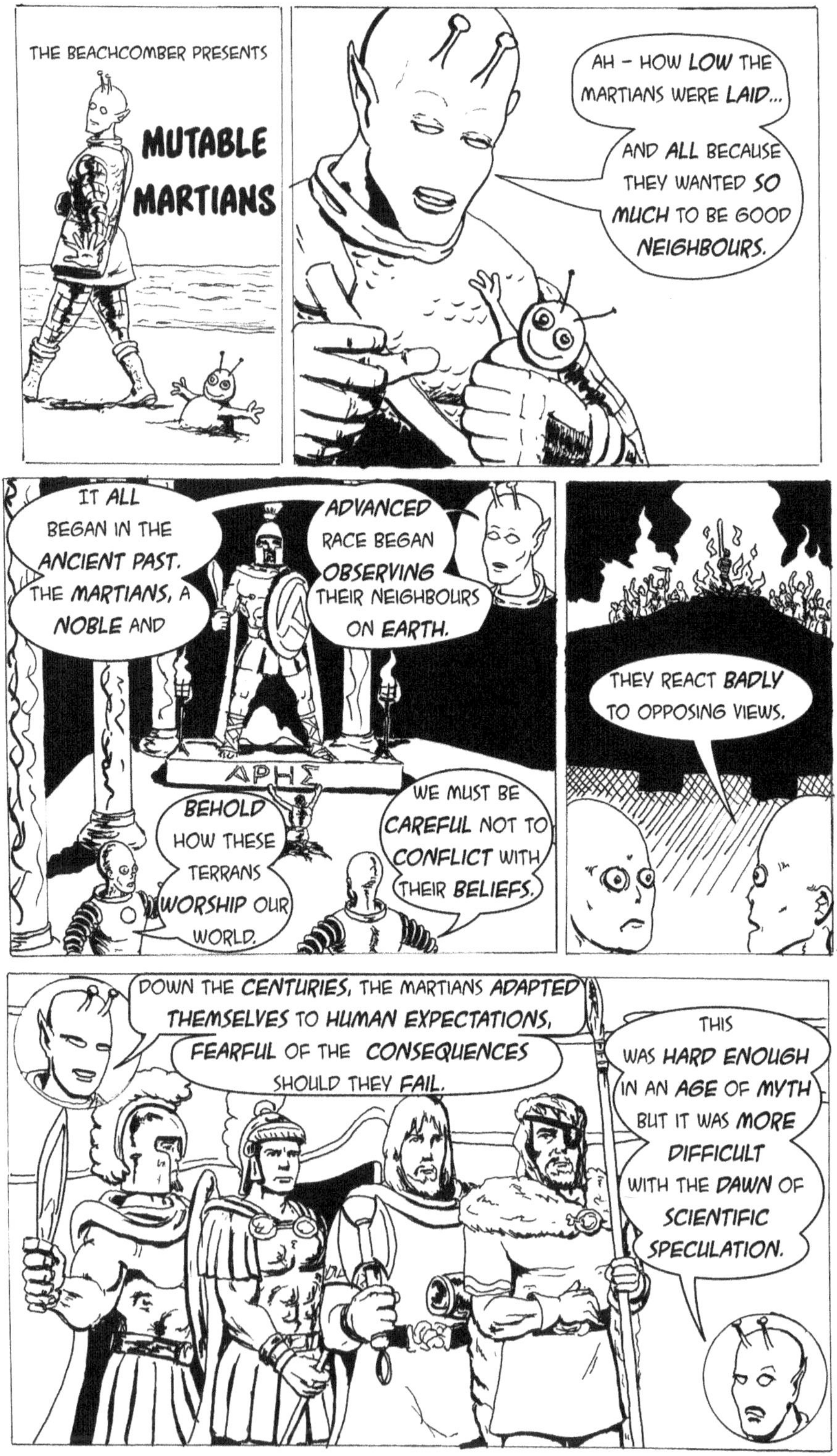

THE BEACHCOMBER PRESENTS
MUTABLE MARTIANS
AH - HOW LOW THE MARTIANS WERE LAID...
AND ALL BECAUSE THEY WANTED SO MUCH TO BE GOOD NEIGHBOURS.
IT ALL BEGAN IN THE ANCIENT PAST. THE MARTIANS, A NOBLE AND
ADVANCED RACE BEGAN OBSERVING THEIR NEIGHBOURS ON EARTH.
ΑΡΗΣ
BEHOLD HOW THESE TERRANS WORSHIP OUR WORLD.
WE MUST BE CAREFUL NOT TO CONFLICT WITH THEIR BELIEFS.
THEY REACT BADLY TO OPPOSING VIEWS.
DOWN THE CENTURIES, THE MARTIANS ADAPTED THEMSELVES TO HUMAN EXPECTATIONS, FEARFUL OF THE CONSEQUENCES SHOULD THEY FAIL.
THIS WAS HARD ENOUGH IN AN AGE OF MYTH BUT IT WAS MORE DIFFICULT WITH THE DAWN OF SCIENTIFIC SPECULATION.

IT ALL STARTED WITH *GIOVANNI SCHIAPARELLI.* SCHIAPARELLI MADE THE *BEST* OBSERVATIONS OF *MARS* IN HIS TIME. HE *MAPPED* THE RED PLANET IN *GREAT DETAIL.*

THEN, IN *1877,* HE MAPPED A NETWORK OF *LINEAR FEATURES* WHICH HE CALLED 'CHANNELS.' THE *ITALIAN* WORD 'CANALI' WAS MISTRANSLATED 'CANALS' IN *ENGLISH* AND SPECULATION BEGAN ABOUT THE *CANAL* BUILDERS.

OF COURSE, NOT WANTING TO *DISAPPOINT,* THE *MARTIANS* TRIED TO *EMULATE* THE POPULAR VIEW.

THEY *BUILT* THE WAR MACHINES OF *H. G. WELLS.*

THEY WERE ALTOGETHER MORE *GLAMOROUS* IN THE TIME OF *EDGAR RICE BURROUGHS.*

THE **20TH CENTURY** STARTED WITH A LOT OF INTERESTING IDEAS. **MARTIAN FASHION JOURNALISTS** COULD REPORT ON THE **NEW FORMS** THAT THE **WRITERS** AND **ARTISTS** OF **EARTH** WOULD **DESIGN** EVERY FEW YEARS.

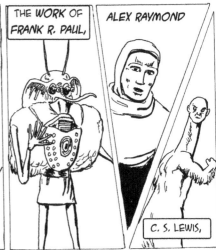

THE **WORK** OF **FRANK R. PAUL,**

ALEX RAYMOND

C. S. LEWIS,

CHUCK JONES.

HOWEVER THE **FUN** WAS **TEMPERED** BY A CERTAIN **WISTFULNESS.**

IN THE **STORIES,** EARTHLING HEROES **VISITED** MARS...

BUT, IN **REALITY,** THEY **NEVER CAME.**

IN THE **SECOND HALF** OF THE **20TH CENTURY,** MARTIANS WERE **NEVER MORE POPULAR.**

YET THE **WEEKLY** CHANGES OF FORM WERE TAKING THEIR **TOLL** ON THE **HAPLESS MARTIANS.**

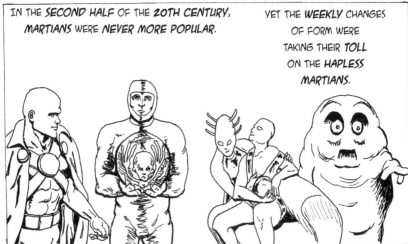

WHILE **BIOLOGISTS** LOOKED AT THE **ENVIRONMENT** OF MARS AND **FAILED TO SEE** HOW THE MARTIANS COULD **SURVIVE** THERE...

THE INGENIOUS **RAY BRADBURY** GUESSED AT THE **TRANSMUTATIVE NATURE** OF THE MARTIANS AND THE **DIFFICULTY** OF **RECOGNISING** THEM...

AND THE **POOR MARTIANS CONTINUED** TO CHANGE TO **PLEASE** THE **EARTHLINGS** WHO **WOULD NOT VISIT.**

THE **GOLDEN AGE** OF EARTH **TELEVISION** PROVED THE **LAST STRAW.**

THERE WERE **MORE MARTIANS** TO **BECOME** THAN THE FLEXIBLE BEINGS COULD **SAFELY ACCOMMODATE.**

AND SOON, THEY WERE **GONE** – RETREATED **BENEATH** THE **SURFACE** TO BECOME THE **SIMPLE ORGANISMS** THAT **EARTH SCIENCE** OF THE DAY **COULD ACCEPT.**

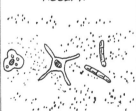

IT'S A **HARD LESSON.** SOMETIMES LETTING OUR **FEAR** MAKE US **SOMETHING** WE ARE **NOT** CAN PROVE **MORE DISASTEROUS** THAN BEING **TRUE** TO **OURSELVES.**

A MARTIAN LIST

H. G. WELLS 'THE WAR OF THE WORLDS'
EDGAR RICE BURROUGHS 'A PRINCESS OF MARS' AND MANY MORE
RAY BRADBURY 'THE MARTIAN CHRONICLES'
FRANK R. PAUL 'THE MAN FROM MARS' IN 'FANTASTIC ADVENTURES' 1939
ALEX RAYMOND 'FLASH GORDON'
C. S. LEWIS 'OUT OF THE SILENT PLANET'
CHUCK JONES 'DUCK DODGERS IN THE 24½ CENTURY' CARTOON SHORT
JOSEPH SAMACHSON AND JOE CERTA 'THE STRANGE EXPERIMENT OF DR. ERDEL' IN 'DETECTIVE COMICS' #225
WILLIAM CAMERON MENZIES 'INVADERS FROM MARS' FEATURE
STAN LEE AND JACK KIRBY 'THE JOKER!' IN 'AMAZING ADVENTURES #5
JOHN L. GREEN 'MY FAVOURITE MARTIAN' SITCOM
GEORGE PAL 'THE WAR OF THE WORLDS' FEATURE
BRIAN HAYLES 'THE ICE WARRIORS' TV EPISODE
GERRY ANDERSON 'THUNDERBIRDS ARE GO' FEATURE AND 'CAPTAIN SCARLET' TV SERIES

SF Caledonia

Monica Burns

That Very Mab
May Kendall and Andrew Lang
Published 1885

This issue's SF Caledonia is a first for two reasons. For one, the book was written in collaboration by two different authors, and secondly, one of the collaborators was female (finally we've found one!) These two writers, May Kendall and Andrew Lang, were already established as writers but joined forces to create a fairy tale satire called *That Very Mab* which they published, at first anonymously, in 1885.

If you recognise the name Mab, then yes, it is indeed that very Mab you're thinking of. She is the Fairy Queen featured in many works of British literature. She originates from Shakespeare's *Romeo and Juliet*, in a speech by Mercutio:

"O, then, I see Queen Mab hath been with you / She is the fairies' midwife, and she comes / In shape no bigger than an agate-stone".

From within this speech is where Kendall and Lang got their title:

"This is that very Mab / That plaits the manes of horses in the night".

Since Shakespeare drew a lot of his material from folklore and old stories, many people debate over the origins of Queen Mab prior to Shakespeare, often pointing to Celtic folklore, particularly the Irish Queen Medb (pronounced *mev* or *maive*). Regardless of her initial origins, she has clearly captured the imagination of many writers and poets after Shakespeare, including Ben Jonson, John Milton and Percy Shelley. So by the time May Kendall and Andrew Lang were writing in 1885, during an era enamoured with fairy stories, it was likely that readers would know exactly who Queen Mab was. Kendall and Lang add to the canon of Queen Mab literature, but they offer us a unique take on her. The story uses the queen of the fairies as a vehicle to satirically

Andrew Lang. Alas, we couldn't source a photograph of May Kendall.

explore the absurdities and contradictions of modern life. The basic premise is that Queen Mab had left Britain long ago because the rise of Puritan Christianity in Britain made the fairies flee. She had resettled in the Polynesian island of Samoa. However, various warring parties of missionaries who invade and disrupt her new home drive Mab back to her roots. Flying upon a seagull, she returns to Britain to see what became of her former kingdom in the years of her absence. At first despondent at the lack of support among her former subjects, the animals and insects, she finds company in a wise but pessimistic owl, who interprets modern civilisation for her. Together, they make a study of analysing issues of science, religion, politics, art and philosophy. This makes up the basic framework for the plot of *That Very Mab*. All that follows are the events which Mab and the Owl see or become involved in, and their discussions about them.

As is often the case in philosophical fantasy and science fiction from the nineteenth century, the novel's characters are not supposed to be three-dimensional people, but operate as archetypes, named only after their profession or a particular character trait. There are characters called only the Poet, the Bishop, the Nihilist and so on, which makes the world seem more like a fairy tale than a real representation of Britain. Kendall and Lang have a knack for making the reader take a second look at what they know of issues like science and politics, and marvel at absurd human fixations.

One contemporary response to the book was mostly favourable. When *That Very Mab* first came out, the critic, science-writer and novelist, Grant Allen, wrote a review in Longman's Magazine (which regularly printed Lang's work, so much so that readers mistook him for the editor). Allen identified the then-anonymous authors as a new writer, claiming that the writing "has a vein of its own; sometimes it is rollicking, sometimes it is plaintive, sometimes it is satirical, sometimes it is mystifying, but always it is clever and always pessimistic."

Allen's review opens with a puzzle on how *That Very Mab* should be categorised on the shelves. He comes to the conclusion:

"If I had to give it a name, I should say it was a satire, but a satire of the most comprehensive catholic description, since it addresses hard knocks to everybody all round with great impartiality, except only owls and fairies. And even the owls have a doubtful time of it."

But more than130 years since the book's publication and Allen's review, there is an extra genre to add to the mix that did not then exist in the way we know it today: science fiction. In a similar way to other novels *SF Caledonia* has looked at so far, categorising nineteenth century novels as science fiction can be dubious at times, given that the genre did not necessarily exist under the definitions we have today. Certainly, *That Very Mab* could be slotted into the fantasy genre quite easily. Little details of fairy magic are sprinkled throughout the book, giving it an authentic fairy story feel to it amid the heavy satire. However, as *SF Caledonia* has discussed before, fantasy doesn't necessarily directly equate with science fiction. As far as I'm concerned, to dub a book science fiction, it has to at least engage with some of the scientific thinking from its time. Though *That Very Mab* does this, it also goes beyond. Throughout the book we are made to believe that the Britain that Mab visits is a parodied version of the real Britain inhabited by Kendall and Lang. However, there is a surprising chapter near the end of the novel in which Parliament are debating colonising the moon "by emigration of the able-bodied unemployed", and we learn that space travel and conquering planets has already been achieved, and there are ongoing turf-wars across the solar system. It is a neat science-fiction addition, where the rest of the book feels more like the late nineteenth century. It emerges from Parliament's discussions that it is not a unified effort by the entire planet Earth to explore space, but individual countries claiming worlds for themselves, so basically extending the petty turf wars from Earth into outer space. MPs discuss "the recent annexation of Mercury by Russia, and the presence in Jupiter of a German emissary".

There are two sections in particular which maintain coincidental foresight. This first is something I feel we might be saying in the future when Earth is forced to colonise the solar system after global warming ruins our own planet: an MP in the Parliamentary debate criticises "the gentleman so highly distinguished for youth and sanity, who has plunged us into oceans of disaster at home and abroad, and, not content with making the world we live in too hot to hold us, intends to make all the planets related to us in the Solar System too hot to hold us, as well."

Another interesting prediction is when Mab and the Owl discuss early robotics: "She said that inanimate objects had no business to be clever, and that, if the mechanicians did not take care, they would shortly invent machines that would conspire together to assassinate them, and then share the profits." Robots going rogue to overthrow their human creators—isn't that a familiar science fiction plot?

Unfortunately, little is known about the particulars of Kendall and Lang's collaboration—who wrote what, and who came up with which idea. However, Kendall and Lang seem to be the perfect literary match for one another. In their individual repertoires, they are both playful, intelligent, unconventional, satirical and they're both interested in the scientific and the fantastic. Whether or not they were friends with one another after *That Very Mab*, they still kept in contact on a literary level at least. May Kendall condensed and adapted *Gulliver's Travels* for the first of Lang's fairy books *The Blue Fairy Book*, in 1889.

Andrew Lang

Of the two authors of *That Very Mab*, more information is known about Andrew Lang. Taking a step away from the unfortunate fact that women in history are often sidelined in favour of their male counterparts, in this case Andrew Lang was the bigger name out of the pair. He was a very well known journalist, novelist, poet and literary critic. Although he is not widely recognised nowadays, to give an idea of his fame and prolificacy during his lifetime, George Bernard Shaw once wrote "the day is empty unless an article by Lang appears". He wrote 80 books as well as his frequent contributions to magazines, poetry and other works. He has no distinct *magnum opus* to his legacy, however he might be best remembered for being the editor of the hugely successful fairy books, published between 1889 and 1913 categorised by the colours of their covers, starting with *The Blue Fairy Book*. He also frequently wrote introductions to books, including all of Walter Scott's *Waverley* novels.

Lang was born in Selkirk in the Scottish Borders in 1844. Both sides of his family had notable ancestors. His maternal grandfather was the infamous Patrick Sellar, the Duke of Sutherland's factor, who played a major role in the Highland Clearances, and his paternal grandfather was sheriff clerk to Sir Walter Scott. Lang went to school at Edinburgh Academy, then studied for his undergraduate degree in the University of St Andrews (where there is now a lecture series named after him), and afterwards went on to study as a postgraduate at the University of Oxford.

Contemporary reports of Lang's personality express mixed feelings. Despite the claim by critic, Theodore Watts-Dunton, that "I never met a man of genius who did not loathe Lang", Lang seemed to have made friends with a lot of famous people, including Sir Arthur Conan Doyle, Rudyard Kipling, JM Barrie and Robert Louis Stevenson. However, his first meeting with Stevenson didn't appear to have gone too well. Stevenson actually wrote this little poem about him, criticising his pretentiousness:

My name is Andrew Lang
Andrew Lang
That's my name
And criticism and cricket is my game
With my eyeglass in my eye
Am not I
Am not I
A la-di da-di Oxford kind of Scot
Am I not?

Whether or not Lang ever knew about the poem, he and Stevenson went on to become life-long friends!

If this description of Lang's writing—"fairy-tales written by an erudite Puck"—is anything to go by, then he must have been a fascinating character to have met. He lived well into his sixties, and died in Banchory, Aberdeenshire in 1912.

May Kendall (Emma Goldworth Kendall)

Sadly, there is not as much information on May Kendall as there is on Andrew Lang. Christened "Emma Goldworth Kendall", she was born the daughter of a Weslyan minister and his wife in Bridlington, Yorkshire, in 1861. It is assumed that she spent most of her life in and around this region, and that she died in 1943 in York. She never married and had a long and prolific career as a poet, writer and social activist. Little is known of her schooling. However, from the amount of knowledge, intelligence and wit in her writing, it would be fair to assume she was well-educated. It is even suggested that she attended Somerville College, Oxford University.

Like many of literature's great ladies, she was a champion for the rights and education of her fellow women. She was among those who the Victorians called a 'New Woman', a term used to describe the new feminist ideal of an educated, independent career woman who exercised control over her own life, which was against the conservative norms of Victorian society. The New Woman's movement had a profound influence on feminism through the nineteenth and well into the twentieth century.

Kendall also took interest in social justice, particularly the working class. She worked closely with the Rowntree family in York (famous for their chocolate and confectionary firm), collaborating on research with Seebohm Rowntree, and publishing a book in 1913 called *How the Labourer Lives: A Study of the Rural Labour Problem*. She eventually gave up her writing to focus her attention on social reform.

The end of May Kendall's life was tragic. When she died in 1943, it was in a public assistance institution and in poverty. Records say that she died with dementia and was buried in an unmarked grave. Her friends and collaborators, the Rowntree family, paid for her funeral.

There is not much to suggest what she was like as a person, but there are certain things you can glean from the little information known about her. Her progressive feminist views, the fact she lived independently and that she did not write under a male pseudonym as many female authors felt the need to in that era, all show that she was astute and independent. Her history of collaboration, particularly with successful men, meant she must have demanded a good deal of respect from them and by her publishers in order to secure these partnerships and make a success of her talents. She was a woman ahead of her time.

There is one other way that May Kendall was ahead of her time—her interest in science fiction. As previously mentioned, in *That Very Mab*, there were science fiction elements, but her interest in it extends further than this. In 1895 she wrote a poem called "A Pure Hypothesis: A Lover, in Four-Dimensioned Space, Describes a Dream" in which, a lover (in an imaginary world of four-dimensioned space) dreams of a world of only three dimension—namely, our own. Here are the first three stanzas.

AH, love, the teacher we decried,
  That erudite professor grim,
In mathematics drenched and dyed,
  Too hastily we scouted him.
He said: "The bounds of Time and Space,
  The categories we revere,
May be in quite another case
  In quite another sphere."

He told us: "Science can conceive
  A race whose feeble comprehension
Can't be persuaded to believe
  That there exists our Fourth Dimension,
Whom Time and Space for ever balk;
  But of these beings incomplete,
Whether upon their heads they walk
  Or stand upon their feet—

"We cannot tell, we do not know,
  Imagination stops confounded;
We can but say 'It may be so,'
  To every theory propounded."

Too glad were we in this our scheme
  Of things, his notions to embrace,—
But—I have dreamed an awful dream
  Of Three-dimensioned Space!

In another poem, *"Woman's Future"*, Kendall urges women to do something extraordinary and break the boundaries of society – to use their imaginations and "invent a new planet". Perhaps it's a little anachronistic to suggest, but it sounds like she's encouraging women to write science fiction! After all, inventing new planets is the bread and butter of many science fiction writers.

On Fashion's vagaries your energies strewing,
Devoting your days to a rug or a screen,
Oh, rouse to a lifework—do something worth doing!
Invent a new planet, a flying machine.
Mere charms superficial, mere feminine graces,
That fade or that flourish, no more you may prize;
But the knowledge of Newton will beam from your faces,
The soul of a Spencer will shine in your eyes.

If May Kendall had been born into our time, with the genre of science fiction at her disposal, who knows what wonderful new planets and flying machines her extraordinary imagination would have invented.

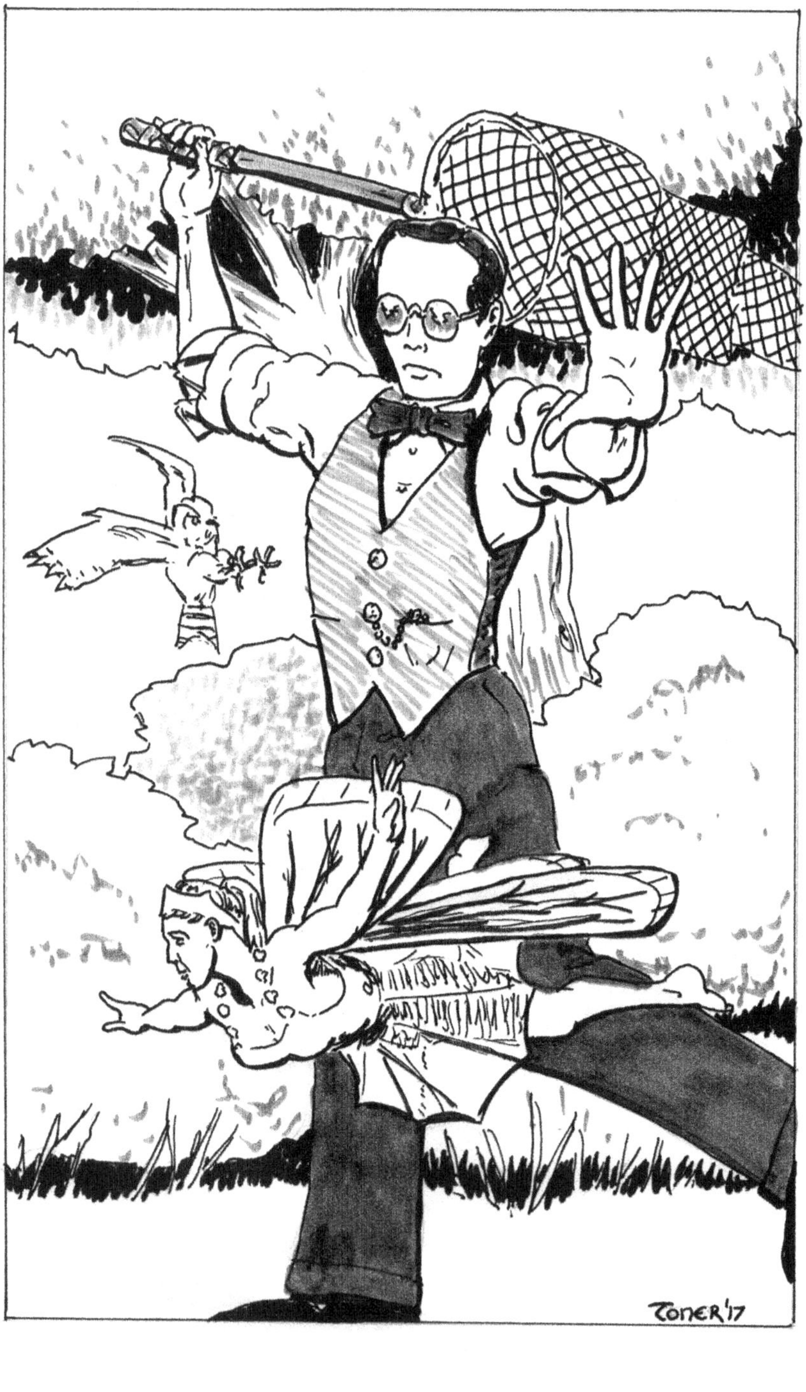
TONER '17

That Very Mab

May Kendall and Andrew Lang

Chapter II—Disillusions

"The time is come," the walrus said, "To talk of many things."

— Alice in Wonderland

Queen Mab found England a good deal altered. There were still fairy circles in the grass; but they were attributed, not to fairy dances, but to unscientific farming and the absence of artificial phosphates. The country did not smell of April and May, but of brick-kilns and the manufacture of chemicals. The rivers, which she had left bright and clear, were all black and poisonous. Water for drinking purposes was therefore supplied by convoys from the Apollinaris and other foreign wells, and it was thought that, if a war broke out, the natives of England would die of thirst. This was not the only disenchantment of Queen Mab. She found that in Europe she was an anachronism. She did not know, at first, what the word meant, but the sense of it gradually dawned upon her. Now there is always something uncomfortable about being an anachronism; but still people may become accustomed to it, and even take a kind of a pride in it, if they are only anachronisms on the right side—so far in the van of the bulk of humanity, for instance, that the bulk of humanity considers them not wholly in their right minds. There must surely be a sense of superiority in knowing oneself a century or two in front of one's fellow-creatures that counterbalances the sense of solitude. Queen Mab had no such consolation. She was an anachronism hundreds of years on the wrong side; in fact, a relic of Paganism.

Of course she was acquainted with the language of all the beasts and birds and insects, and she counted on their befriending her, however much men had changed. Her brief experience of modern sailors and missionaries, whether English or German, had indeed convinced her that men were, even now, far from perfection. But it was a crushing blow to find that all the beasts were traitors, and all the insects. If it had not been for the loyal birds she would have gone back to Polynesia at once; but they flocked faithfully to her standard, led by the Owl, the wisest of all feathered things, who had lived too long, and had too much good feeling to ignore fairies, though he was, perhaps, just a little of a prig.

※

The Owl talked a good deal about the low moral tone of the human race in this respect, and was pessimistic about it, failing to perceive that higher types of organisms always like to signify their superiority over lower ones by shooting them, or otherwise making their lives a burden. The Owl, however, was a very talented bird, and one felt that even his fallacies were a mark of attainments beyond those common to his race. He had read and thought a great deal, and could tell Queen Mab about almost anything she asked him. This was pleasant, and she sat with him on a very high oak in Epping Forest above a pond, and made observations. It was lovely weather, just the weather for sitting on the uppermost branches of a great oak, and she began to feel like herself again. She had forgotten to put her invisible cloak on; but as she was only half a foot high, and dressed in green, no one saw her up there. Having reached the Forest at night, she had met as yet with few British subjects; but the Owl explained that she would see many hundreds of them before the day was over, coming to admire Nature.

"And does nobody believe in fairies?" sighed Queen Mab.

"No, or at least hardly anyone. A few of the children, perhaps, and a very, very few grown-up people—persons who believe in Faith-healing and Esoteric Buddhism, and Thought-

reading, and Arbitration, and Phonetic Spelling, can believe in anything, except what their mothers taught them on their knees. All of these are in just now."

"What do you mean by 'in'?"

"In fashion; and what is fashionable is to be believed in. Why, you might be the fashion again," said the Owl excitedly. "Why not? And then people would believe in you. What a game it all is, to be sure! But the fashions of this kind don't last," the bird added; "They get snuffed out by the scientific men."

"Tell me exactly who the scientific men are," said the fairy. "I have heard so much about them since I came."

"They are the men," sighed the Owl, "Who go about with microscopes, that is, instruments for looking into things as they are not meant to be looked at and seeing them as they were never intended to be seen. They have put everything under their microscopes, except stars and First Causes; but they had to take telescopes to the stars, because they were so far off ; and First Causes they examined by stethoscopes, which each philosopher applied to his own breast. But, as all the breasts are different, they now call First Causes no business of theirs. They make most things their business, though. They have had a good deal of trouble with

"Ah, he was a great man, Shakespeare, almost too large for a microscope!" said the Owl reflectively.

the poets, because the poets liked to put themselves and their critics under their own microscopes, and they objected to the microscopes of the scientific men. You know what poets are?"

"Yes, indeed," said Queen Mab, feeling at home on the subject. "I have forgotten a good many things, I daresay, with living in Polynesia, but not about the poets. I remember Shakespeare very well, and Herrick is at my court in the Pacific."

"Ah, he was a great man, Shakespeare, almost too large for a microscope!" said the Owl reflectively. "They have put him under a good many since he died, however, especially German lenses. But we were talking about the philosophers—another name for the scientific men—the men who don't know everything."

"I should have thought they did," said Queen Mab.

"No," said the Owl. "It is the theologians who know everything, or at least they used to do so. But lately it has become such a mark of mental inferiority to know everything, that they are always casting it in each other's teeth. It has grown into a war-cry with both parties: '*You think you know everything*' and it is hard for a bird to find out how it all began and what it is all about. I believe it sprang originally out of the old microscope difficulty. The philosophers wanted to put theology under the microscope, and the theologians excommunicated microscopes, and said theology ought never to be looked at except with the Eye of Faith. Now the philosophers are borrowing an eye of Faith from the theologians, and adding it on to their own microscope like another lens, and they have detected a kind of Absolute, a sort of a Something, the Higher Pantheism. I could never tell you all about it, and I don't even know whether they have really put theology under the microscope, or only theologians."

"Well," said Mab mournfully at last, "I must go back to Samoa; there is too much mystery here for me. But who is that?"

She broke off suddenly, for a new and mysterious object had just entered the glade, and was advancing towards the pool.

"Hush!" said the Owl. "Do take care. It is a scientific man—a philosopher."

It was a tall, thin personage, with spectacles and a knapsack, and what reminded Queen Mab of a small green landing-net, but was really intended to catch butterflies. He came up to the pond, and she imagined he was going to fish ; but no, he only unfastened his knapsack and took some small phials and a tin box out of it. Then, bending down to the edge of the water, he began to skim its surface cautiously with a ladle and empty the contents into one of his phials. Suddenly a look of delight came into his face, and he uttered a cry— "Stephanoceros!"

Queen Mab thought it was an incantation, and, trembling with fear, she relaxed her hold of the bough and fell. Not into the pond! She had wings, of course, and half petrified with horror though she was, she yet fluttered away from that stagnant water. But alas, in the very effort to escape, she had caught the eye of the Professor; he sprang up—pond, animalcule all forgotten in the chase of this extraordinary butterfly. The fairy's courage failed her: her presence of mind vanished, and the wild gyrations of the Owl, who, too late, realised the peril of his companion, only increased her confusion. In another moment she was a prisoner under the butterfly-net. Beaming with delight, the philosopher turned her carefully into the tin box, shut the lid and hastened home, too much enraptured with his prize even to pause to secure the valuable Stephanoceros.

But Queen Mab had fainted, as even fairies must do at such a terrible crisis; and perhaps it was as well that she had, for the professor forbore to administer chloroform, under the impression that his lovely captive had completely succumbed. He put her, therefore, straight into a tall glass bottle, and began to survey her carefully, walking round and round. Truly, he had never seen such a remarkable butterfly.

CHAPTER III.

THE ORIGIN OF RELIGION.

"Rough draughts of Man's Beginning God!"

—Swinburne

When Queen Mab recovered consciousness she heard the sound of violent voices in the room before she opened her eyes which she did half hoping to find herself the victim of some terrible delusion. But the sight of the professor, standing not a yard away, brought a fatal conviction to her heart. It was too true. Was there ever a more undesirable position for a fairy, accustomed to perfect freedom, and nourished by honey and nectar, than to be closely confined in a tall bottle, with smooth hard slippery walls that she could not pierce, and nothing to live upon but a glass-stopper! It was absurd; but it was also terrible. How fervently she wished, now, that the missionaries had never come to Polynesia.

But the professor was not alone, two of his acquaintances were there—a divine veering towards the modern school, and a poet—the ordinary poet of satire and Mr. Besant's novels, with an eye-glass, who held that the whole duty of poets at least was to transfer the meanderings of the inner life, or as much of them as were in any degree capable of transmission, to immortal foolscap. Unfortunately, as he observed with a mixture of pride and regret, the workings of his soul were generally so ethereal as to baffle expression and comprehension; and, he was wont to say, mixing up metaphors at a great rate, that he could only stand, like the High Priest of the Delphic oracle, before the gates of his inner life, to note down such fragmentary utterances as 'foamed up from the depths of that divine chaos' for the benefit of inquiring minds with a preference for the oracular. He added that cosmos was a condition of grovelling minds, and that while the thoughts, faculties, and emotions of an ordinary member of society might fitly be summed up in the epithet 'microcosm', his own nature could be appropriately described only by that of 'microchaos'. In which opinionthe professor always fully coincided. With the two had entered the professor's little boy, a motherless child of eight, who walked straight up to the bottle.

> **"...the workings of his soul were generally so ethereal as to baffle expression and" comprehension..."**

No sooner did the child's eyes light on the vessel than a curious thing occurred. He fell down on his knees, bowed his head, and held up his hands.

"Great Heavens!" cried the professor, forgetting himself, "What do I behold! My child is praying (a thing he never was taught to do), and praying to a green butterfly! Hush! Hush!" the professor went on, turning to his friends. "This is terrible, but most important. The child has never been allowed to hear anything about the supernatural—his poor mother died when he was in the cradle—and I have scrupulously shielded him from all dangerous conversation. There is not a prayer-book in the house, the maids are picked Agnostics, from advanced families, and I am quite certain that my boy has never even heard of the existence of a bogie."

The poet whistled: the divine took up his hat, and, with a pained look, was leaving the room.

"Stop, stop!" cried the professor, "He is doing something odd."

The child had taken out of his pocket certain small black stones of a peculiar shape. So absorbed was he that he never noticed the presence of the men. He kissed the stones and arranged them in a curious pattern on the floor, still kneeling, and keeping his eye on

Mab in her bottle. At last he placed one strangely shaped pebble in the centre, and then began to speak in a low, trembling voice, and in a kind of cadence:

"Oh! you that I have tried to see,

Oh! you that I have heard in the night,

Oh! you that live in the sky and the water;

Now I see you, now you have come:

Now you will tell me where you live,

And what things are, and who made them.

Oh Dala, these stones are yours;

These are the *goona* stones I find,

And play with when I think of you.

Oh Dala, be my friend, and never leave me

Alone in the dark night."

"As I live, it's a religious service, the worship of a green butterfly!" said the professor. At his voice the child turned round, and seeing the men, looked very much ashamed of himself.

"Come here, my dear old man," said the professor to the child, who came on being called. "What were you doing?—who taught you to say all those funny things?"

The little fellow looked frightened. "I didn't remember you were here," he said; "They are things I say when I play by myself."

"And who is Dala?"

The boy was blushing painfully. "Oh, I didn't mean you to hear, it's just a game of mine. I play at there being somebody I can't see, who knows what I am doing; a friend."

"And nobody taught you, not Jane or Harriet?"

Now Harriet and Jane were the maids.

"You never saw anybody play at that kind of game before?"

"No," said the child, "Nobody ever."

"Then," cried the professor, in a loud and blissful voice, "We have at last discovered the origin of religion. It isn't Ghosts. It isn't the Infinite. It is worshipping butterflies, with a service of fetich stones. The boy has returned to it by an act of unconscious inherited memory, derived from Palaeolithic Man, who must, therefore, have been the native of a temperate climate, where there were green lepidoptera. Oh, my friends, what a thing is inherited memory! In each of us there slumber all the impressions of all our predecessors, up to the earliest Ascidian. See how the domesticated dog," cried the professor, forgetting that he was not lecturing in Albemarle Street, "See how the domesticated dog, by inherited memory, turns round on the hearthrug before he curls up to sleep! He is unconsciously remembering the long grasses in which his wild ancestors dwelt. Also observe this boy, who has retained an unconscious recollection of the earliest creed of prehistoric man. Behold him instinctively, and I may say automatically, cherishing fetich stones (instead of marbles, like other boys) and adoring that green insect in the glass bottle! Oh Science," he added rapturously, "What will Mr. Max Müller say now? The Infinite! Bosh, it's a butterfly!"

"It is my own Dala, come to play with me," said the boy.

"It is a fairy," exclaimed the poet, examining Mab through his eyeglass. This he said, not that he believed in fairies any more than publishers believed in him, but partly because it was a pose he affected, partly to 'draw' the professor.

The professor replied that fairies were unscientific, and even unthinkable, and the divine declared that they were too heterodox even for the advanced state of modern theology, and had been condemned by several councils, which is true. And the professor ran through all the animal kingdoms and sub-kingdoms very fast, and proved quite conclusively, in a perfect cataract of polysyllables, that fairies didn't belong to any of them. While the professor was recovering breath, the divine observed, in a somewhat aggrieved tone, that he for his part found men and women enough for him, and too much sometimes. He also wished to know whether, if his talented but misguided friend required something ethereal, angels were not sufficient, without his having recourse to Pagan mythology; and whether he considered Pagan mythology suitable to the pressing needs of modern society, with a large surplus female population, and to the adjustment of the claims of reason and religion.

The poet replied, "Oh, don't bother me with your theological conundrums. I give it up. See here, I am going to write a sonnet to this creature, whatever it is. *Fair denizen—* !"

"Of a glass bottle!" interrupted the professor somewhat rudely, and the divine laughed.

"No. *Of deathless ether, doomed.*"

"And that reminds me," said the professor, turning hastily, "I must examine it under the microscope carefully, while the light lasts."

"Oh father!" cried the child, "Don't touch it, it is alive!"

"Nonsense!" said the professor, "It is as dead as a door-nail. Just reach me that lens."

He raised the glass stopper unsuspiciously, then turned to adjust his instrument And even as he turned his captive fled.

"There!" cried the boy. Like a flash of sunshine, Queen Mab darted upwards and floated through the open window. They saw her hover outside a moment, then she was gone—back into her deathless ether.

"I told you so!" exclaimed the poet, startled by this incident into a momentary conviction of the truth of his own theory.

Interview: Jane Yolen

Jane Yolen has been called the Hans Christian Andersen of America. She has written over 300 books, many poems (including SF poetry), won numerous awards including the Nebula (twice), and is a past president of SFWA (Science Fiction Writers of America). She splits her time between her home in Massachusetts and her house in Scotland.
Here she is in email conversation with Russell Jones

Russell Jones: Can you tell us a little about your relationship(s) with science fiction?

Jane Yolen: My relationship began way back in the 1950's when I discovered the Groff Conklin anthologies. Even then I was more interested in character, story than the actual science. A failure, some might say. But if it is that, it has stuck with me till now when I am <mumble mutter> years old.
I am basically a folklorist with an abiding interest in the natural sciences rather than the space or cutting-edge sciences. My reading (and my writing) follow this interest. Tell me about fireflies mating rituals and I will follow you anywhere. Give me a Mars Rover and I want to know about

what it finds. But talk to me about equations, and only if it is a metaphor, can I get hot for it. Maybe it's why I married a scientist. I could always ask for easier explanations from him.

RJ: It sounds like you're more interested in the speculative possibilities of science for storytelling purposes, rather than being tied into the accuracy of the science itself. With that in mind, do you think art, and particularly science fiction, has a responsibility to address or challenge contemporary concerns?

JY: I think that all art has a responsibility to itself and to speak the True. That True is often not actual, but something deeper. Emily Dickinson wrote:

Tell all the truth but tell it slant —
Success in Circuit lies
Too bright for our infirm Delight
The Truth's superb surprise
As Lightning to the Children eased
With explanation kind
The Truth must dazzle gradually
Or every man be blind —

It's my mantra. And after all--what is actual is but an agreed upon truth. Is the world flat, round, ovoid? You can probably find people who believe in any of these. Is the ruling god Jehovah/Christ? Gaia? The Flying Spaghetti Monster? None of the above? I can show you people who believe. And how many weather deniers can you fit on the head of a pin? My sole goal is to write well, tell a great story, make my character actually stride across the pages, to write a perfect poem, tell the True. (Note I don't say Tell the Truth.) But of course, because I am a white Jewish woman of the 20th and 21st centuries, my take on the True will be different from a Man of that time or a person of a different color or upbringing or gender preference or. . .So the secondary part of my writing is to write well enough so that I do not just preach to the choir, but enlarge and engage the choir.
But first I have to write well.
And sometimes I do.

RJ: You raise Emily Dickinson's "tell it slant" (a popular poetry mantra now), which leads nicely into the realms of verse. You're a widely published poet as well as prose writer; do you feel that poetry has anything to add to science fiction which prose cannot? Is there anything which science fiction adds to the genre of poetry?

JY: Ah, you are baiting me! Of course I feel both things. Poetry's metaphor can explain and enlarge upon the facts of fiction; it can be a take-away from that science thing you are learning; a mnemonic to aid your memory; and a depth charge as well. Recently a poem of mine, "The Day After" became the heading for a newsletter sent to people interested in Lynn Margulis' work on the Gaia Theory and evolution geography which—while truly science—is a very science fictional field itself.
And of course there is a lot of sf poetry out there and a Science Fiction Poetry Association to keep

poets abreast of markets, publish small essays on the field, and hand out SFPA awards called the Rhyslings and Dwarf Stars.

If you think about it, even non-sf poets use metaphors that are strikingly like science fiction: Yeats' "The Second Coming" is a perfect example.

RJ: You mention the SFPA, for which you are one of the Grandmasters. Could you tell us a little about this role, and your views on the potential values of establishing science fiction societies and communities?

JY: The SFPA Grandmaster is an honorary role (as is the World Fantasy Assn. Grandmaster, which I also am.) All I get are bragging rights. […] However, I *have* been president of SFWA (Science Fiction Writers of America) and on advisory committees for that organization as well, and there you do work, and strategize when asked, and have a bully pulpit to speak to the outside world. I was the second women to hold that office.

What can science fiction societies and communities do? Sometimes it seems we just crab and carp a lot, and other animal metaphors. But the best of them become second homes for fans and writers and illustrators. There we can share trade secrets, read one another's work, set up art shows, hold movie parties, conventions, workshops. The best supporter of the arts is--as always--the artists. The best voices for sf are those who read and write it. But we need to be inclusive, not exclusive, not shoving out the Muggles, cold-shouldering the wannabes, or turning on them like rabid puppies. It is imperative to bring the newer sf folk to the fire and let them learn how to stoke the flames.

RJ: that's good to hear, and those are some of Shoreline of Infinity's mission objectives: to bring new people to SF, to allow new writers to speak and flourish. On that line - as an Old Hand (at the writing, no comments on age here!), are there any books (from your now 360-odd published) which didn't make it to print but you wished they had? Or any which were published which you wish hadn't been?

JY: There are always regrets, mostly about early books, that I wish I could do over. And in fact, the very first one that I published (with McKay) I did. That early book (1963) was *Pirates in Petticoats* and I completely rewrote it, and it was published by Charlesbridge as *Sea Queens* in 2008. In the in-between time, a lot more had been published about female pirates than I had unearthed in the earlier book. But female pirates became an obsession with me from then on, as were strong young women. You can find many of them in my sf/fantasy books.

As for books not yet published (and not yet even taken provisionally by a publisher), three stand out, all fantasy rather than a hard sf: *Finding Baba Yaga* which is a verse novel for teens about a modern runaway who becomes one of Baba Yaga's legions of feisty girls. *The Sea Dragon of Fife,* is a middle grade novel about the R&A Royal and Ancient

Monster Hunters a hundred years ago in Fife, who trap monsters but are almost out-manned and outwitted by a nasty sea dragon and her son. And *The Last Tsar's Dragons* (written with Adam Stemple, my son) which first came out as a novella for adults and we want to turn into an adult novel, about Tsar Nicholas, Stalin, Rasputin and red dragons.

Plus about 35 picture books and poetry collections.

And about 25 books under contract, all but 1 of them written.

RJ: I'm very interested in your thoughts on "strong young women" in your books, and in literature more generally. We are slowly beginning to see more multidimensional, well written women characters in SF on the television too. Can you tell us about the strong young women in your work, and whether you feel there's been any change in the presentation of women in literature during your career?

JY: I have been writing so many strong young women in my books over the years that these days I am actually getting pushback from parents to include more strong boys! A sort of backhanded compliment I suppose.

Part of that in children's books was the automatic assumption that girls read all the times but the more active boys (note the double assumption) don't read, and the automatic corollary: that girls will read books with boys as heroes but boys will not read books with girl heroes.

Nowadays there are more books about strong women in history, strong princesses, strong female astronauts, strong, female bridge builders or explorers, etc. But there are still many literary glass ceilings yet to be broken. I will continue to try and help crack them wide.

Some of my fantasy/sf books with strong females: Sister Light/Sister Dark trilogy; The Seelie Wars trilogy, Snow in Summer, Not One Damsel in Distress, The Devil's Arithmetic, Except the Queen, among others.

RJ : Keep breaking those glass ceilings, please! I recall a recent online discussion about (I think, correct me if I'm wrong) a lack of male dinosaurs in one of your books. Do you find that you have to defend your work often, particularly given how widely read your books are? It seems as though it would be impossible to escape criticism - how do you deal with that?

JY: First of all, it was a lack of FEMALE dinosaurs in those books that has been a problem. And honestly, given the preponderance of active female v. males in my books, the critics should have considered the overall balance.

Also, the first book (I never thought of it as the start of a series, just the one book) was explicitly written for the editor's son. She'd said to me, "My son Robbie hates to go to bed and loves dinosaurs, can you write something for him?" As I'd had two sons like that--my daughter was never a problem at bedtime—I had my own models for those naughty dinos.

But the problem about active girls in children's books exists. And like everything else in the world, redressing that one problem brings up another. Nothing is perfectly balanced. I began a poem that Asimov's will be publishing, this way:

Balance
"Balance, as Miss Armstrong often reminded. .
.was a gift from the Lord to those who deserved it."

--Gregory Maguire, After Alice
Balance, Balanchine proposed belonged alone to primas.

The ownership of rich folks the bankers all believe.

Balance is the center of the sane,The doctors tell us.

A state of equilibrium, the sculptors' hands deceive. . .

I believe that we may try to achieve as much parity in children's literature, but will always fail. As in life, it's the trying that's important. And perhaps I--like many others--are extremely trying whilst doing so. <Winks>

RJ: Are you, then, quite aware of your audience (or their parents!) during the writing process? Maybe you can tell us a little about how your books tend to go from "Idea" to "Book" -

JY: I don't actually think of audience directly when writing. At this point (almost 60 years into my writing career) I just write what interests me and then look at it and think about audience after.

One example: over the years I've written a bunch of poems about female characters from myth, legend, and folklore: characters such as Medusa, Baba Yaga, Penelope, resulka, sirens, selchies, Lilith. Some of the poems have being accepted and/or published in adult magazines such as Asimov's, Mythic Delirium, Apex& Abyss, or in anthologies--both adult and Young Adult.

About a year ago I realized I had enough poems for a collection. But 1: Knowing how difficult selling an adult book of poetry is 2: How good YA can cross over into adult, and 3: That I am better known in the children's/ YA field, I began to shape this into a collection for YA readers.

RJ: I'd never really thought about YA poetry as a classification. Can you tell us about your interests in children and YA readers—what draws you towards them? Do you feel that myth, fantasy and sci-fi are particularly suited to those groups in particular?

JY: First of all, I think the majority of poetry has elements of fantasy in it. After all, aren't metaphor and simile kinds of fantasy? Think of how many fantastical elements are here in this familiar poem by Robert Burns:

O my Luve is like a red, red rose
That's newly sprung in June;
O my Luve is like the melody
That's sweetly played in tune.

His love is not *actually* a rose,

in June or any other month. Nor red. Nor is she an *actual* melody. Though any good fantasy writer could take it further into floral-filia or a musical muse love affair. The speaker is not going to be around till the rocks melt and the seas go dry. But it's a good premise for a dystopian romance novel. And don't get me started on the trek novel about a walk of ten thousand miles.

More seriously, I fell into children's books and writing fiction and verse for young readers back in the early '60s (the date not my age!) and love being here. But before that (and after as well) I have written for adults. I think the borders blur for me. And sometimes for my readers as well. I am a classic crossover writer. And in some ways I am still that occasionally acerbic, moody, yet entirely optimistic (in a pessimistic kind of way) teenager I was years ago. And my poetry reflects all those facets. Old coal into diamonds (I hope).

RJ: Do you think such optimism is justified? One might call it naive (not I!). SF can rarely cope with utopias but there's also a propensity to slip too far into dystopia. More than ever (recent political events in particular), I wonder if pragmatic optimism is required, or whether we need to bear witness to the darkness, which may not always have a happy end.

JY: Well, I am not entirely optimistic. Just that my natural (Jewish) pessimism is well tempered by my New York inborn snark, my New England bedrock work ethic, and the educated woman's reluctant hope. Oh and softened by my adopted Scottish phrase, "Aye, we'll pay for it!" whenever anything truly wonderful happens.
LOL

RJ: A lot happened during the course of this interview. Brexit, Trump - to name but two behemoths. Does your optimism remain strong for the future? To close our chat: what's in store for your readers in 2017 and beyond?

JY: First--you can get my new book of adult political poems *Before/The Vote/After* from Levellers Press.

Support the arts, an arts collective, and get to hear hearty liberal poems, with an intro by our own ACLU Western Mass. head, attorney Bill Newman. Yes, sometimes anger (and fear) drive my poems. But surprisingly some of them are humorous, too!

Then I am speaking all across the USA: Florida, South Carolina, Boston, New York for starters, and teaching my Picture Book Boot Camp as well.

I have five or six new books out besides the political poetry book, depending upon publishers schedules, and any number of poems scheduled in magazines and journals.

And I'm trying to date. As I am 77, this is amusing, frustrating, and exciting in equal measure. Having a hard time finding a man of appropriate age able to keep up with me! _____

Multiverse
Russell Jones

This issue's MultiVerse is a little different. It's a Jane Yolen special, offering more of her verse to sink your fangs into, partly as an accompaniment to her author interview. But let's concentrate on the poems in this issue, each of which takes something real and twists it to discuss the nature of reality and perception—which may be particularly important in the current and approaching alt-fact and post-truth world.

"Milk from a Cockroach" takes its leap from a real-life scientific discovery and imagines the retirement of cows, coconuts, goats and mares as the milk industry is revolutionised by the mass production of cockroach milk. Tasty. Kafka fans will notice the nod to "Metamorphosis" in Yolen's playful suggestion that the milk may transform the drinker. This takes "you are what you eat" to another level!

"The Metric of Space" discusses the outwards or inwards approach we take to examining life. One might ask, "What's the point of space travel?" and in this poem Yolen explores the limits of an insular life and what becomes of us when we give up on our dreams. The voyage not taken might contort us more than we might expect.

"Spider Rain" makes a real (but uncanny) event seem science fictional, with an added sprinkle of horror to anyone suffering from arachnophobia. It blends myth and reality, unsettling the notion of truth and our human desire for myth-making.

Finally, "Stardust" makes a near-romantic link between the universe and its observers. Scientific fascinations create a kind of lustful magic to those who pursue them, and the poem is perhaps implying that the vital essence of understanding the universe lies somewhere between scientific fact and personal attraction and/or perception: "our bodies' own galaxies."

Milk from a Cockroach: or Gregor's Revenge

"An international team of scientists has just
sequenced a protein crystal located in the
midgut of cockroaches."- http://www.sciencealert.com

The old cow, retired in grass,
thinks mournfully of milk parlors.
The coconut, past its prime
sulks ungracious on the tree.
Goats and mares counsel one another,
plan insurrections they never pull off.
But the smart money deals
in cockroach futures,
the production of caloric
bug juice protein supplement.
Added bonus—perhaps you will live forever,
or at least scuttle under counters
to escape the light.

The Metric of Space

"The universe is connected and alive and we are a part of the metric of space." - Nassim Haramein

My metrics have more to do with houses
than constellations. I measure
with a smaller stick.

Need of additional closets
is the space that now concerns me.
Consider yourself warned.

I have a small mind where space
is concerned. Once I believed
we would travel the universes.

I signed up for one of those jaunts.
That was when I was connected and alive.
Now NASA is but a pimple

on the backside of a budget equation.
Space travel happens only
in movies and books.

Since my ticket never got punched,
I've retreated to smaller spaces,
inner spaces.

I claim my metric,
my planet, my universes,
in my poems.

YMMV: Your mileage may vary.

Spider Rain

If it hadn't happened in Goulburn
or earlier in Wagga Wagga,
this angel hair falling from the sky
would seem a cosmic prank.

Like crop circles, Nessie, Yetis,
the footprints of unicorns,
those little heart-shaped trails
made of human desire.

But this story is true, as spiders,
slow on the ground, migrate
by the thousands, hauling up
from underground cities.

Weaving shrouds,
that shawl trees, blanket grass,
flag tall buildings, decorate
even a stunned man's beard.

They fling snag lines into the air,
arachnid *Wings of Blue*,
letting the wind flag them
across the silk roads.

Stardust

"We are in the universe and the universe is in us."
- Neil deGrasse Tyson

I see him now, tall, stately, that dark star
of the planetarium, waving his arms
in time to the music of the seventies.

His robe is filled with motes,
enchanter's hat straining upward.
We are pulled into his orbit.

Not magic, not the charlatan's hand.
Science guides his links and arcs
as he leads us through the maze of sky

into our bodies' own galaxies.

Jane Yolen

Noise and Sparks 4:
The Work of the Heart

Ruth EJ Booth

*"You are not obligated to complete the work,
nor are you free to abandon it."*

—The Talmud

These are the proverbial interesting times for writers of
speculative fiction. As tellers of truth, but not facts, it's disturbing
to watch those who'd have us live in fear of our friends and
neighbours twist those facts to fit such hate-filled falsehoods. But,
as Ursula Le Guin notes, Science Fiction and Fantasy cannot be
confused with lies.[1] The responsibility of the artist is to respond in
kind: to tell the truth, encourage empathy for the oppressed, and
show a way out of the darkness—if not, a little light for a while.
Art becomes even more vital in times when the truth is obscured.

Yet, this also is when making that art becomes so much harder.
For those trapped by greed and ignorance, their health, livelihoods
and families take precedence over creativity. Meanwhile, those
outside can only watch the suffering of loved ones played
out on social media. What were once havens of community

and escapism for us all become litanies of pain, catalogues of tragedies that never had to happen. To engage with it all is to stay informed—but risk harassment, or burn out. To disengage is to allow yourself to heal—but risk cutting yourself off from friends and family, and miss the chance to speak out against the next curtailment of our rights.

Some writers seem to thrive in these times, keeping positive and sharing passionate polemic that raises resistance to glorious art. Others retreat into the work, their created worlds offering the respite that they and their readers so badly need. As cabaret satirists The Creative Martyrs pointed out at their January Sinister Wink show, "we must stay strong, for we are the lucky ones, and there are people who need us."[2] But it's not always that easy. In the face of such willful, relentless hate, it's hard to feel like anything we do matters.

I think a lot about Mervyn Peake these days. Peake was an enthusiastic World War II conscript, despite being so unsuited to soldiering, he was demoted to writing signs for the officers' lavatories. I think of his grotesque 'Self-portrait' of Hitler, of his proposed propaganda leaflet of art to be attributed to the Fuhrer.[3] Of how he repeatedly applied and failed to become a war artist, eventually had a mental breakdown and was invalided out of the army. It's a cheap dig to say he should have picked his opportunities better. Peake wanted to contribute. He just couldn't.

Peake's 'Self-portrait' betrays empathy for Hitler.[4] What might seem counter-intuitive for a willing soldier, for a writer, makes perfect sense: in the business of making things up and writing them down, making our creations as real as possible is paramount. If her reader doesn't believe in a storyteller's characters, she's in big trouble. Likewise, sympathy with her reader allows a storyteller to speak to them. But more than this, it is the bedrock of creativity itself.

Terri Windling's blog, *Myth and Moor*, recently drew attention to 'It all Turns on Affection,' Wendell Berry's treatise on imagination and a more conserving economy.[5] For Berry, imagination encompasses the full scope of the verb "to see," embracing all attributes of an object. Berry believes this full seeing enables sympathy with those with whom we share a place—as opposed to regarding them as mere unimaginable statistics—and that this affectionate imagination is essential to the creation of art.

Peake also saw imagination as entwined with love and the

heart. In examining his creative process, Peter Winnington explains that, for Peake, the heart responds to emotion, which the imagination answers in turn. Imagination cannot substitute for the heart—without it, any creation of the imagination is mechanical, conventional.[6] In other words, you can't write something true if your heart's not in it.

For those who feel unable to write the hopeful message these times call for, this may seem unhelpful. But Berry notes that imagination also carries knowledge to the heart. In the act of imagination that goes into reading a story, then, the reader absorbs the empathy woven into the work at creation. Studies have shown that reading does increase empathy—empathy that is badly needed in times of hate.[7]

This empathetic resistance may come from unlikely quarters. In Peake's 'Self-portrait' we see the fascist dictator of the Third Reich reduced to a reflection in a mirror. Peake forces us to empathize with the man's weariness, the panic in his eyes. Instead of fearing Hitler, we pity him: this is not a monster, but a man. And, as a man, he is weak and fallible, so defeatable—a more subversive stance than may be imagined from the idea of a portrait.

The artist's resistance, then, lies not only in the 'what' of the art we make, but the 'how.' In enabling empathy through imagination, artists encourage a more caring, conserving community. This is why art is so vital to human society. Indeed, Berry believes this process is as important to the arts of economy and domestic life as high culture. Moreover, this empathetic creation is just as vital for the artist. In developing our own empathy, we realise that those who seem to be thriving in times of crisis may be struggling just as much as we are. And perhaps they need the gift of art too.

Peake states one further condition for creative imagination: silence, so we may hear the heart beating—"the sound of the imagination at work." In other words, it's as important to take a break from the world to heal as it is to engage. Perhaps this is what the Creative Martyrs meant about staying strong. To be free to make the art we choose is to be incredibly lucky. And we cannot deny there are people who need this. Ourselves as much as anyone else.

1   Danuta Kean, *Ursula Le Guin rebuts charge that science fiction is 'alternative fact'*, The Guardian, https://www.theguardian.com/books/2017/feb/03/ursula-le-guin-rebuts-charge-that-science-fiction-is-alternative-fact, [accessed 9th February 2017].

2   *The Sinister Wink*, The Bungo-Lo, 29th January 2017.

3   *Mervyn Peake's war paintings unveiled by National Archives*, The Guardian, https://www.theguardian.com/uk/2011/jul/22/mervyn-peake-paintings-national-archives, [accessed 9th February 2017].

4   Sebastian Peake, *The Hitler Portfolio*, The Mervyn Peake Blog, http://mervynpeake.blogspot.co.uk/2011/07/hitler-portfolio.html, [accessed 9th February 2017].

5   Terri Windling., *A neighborly, kind, and conserving economy*, Myth and Moor, http://www.terriwindling.com/blog/2016/12/wendell-berry.html [accessed 9th February 2017]. For the full lecture, see https://www.neh.gov/about/awards/jefferson-lecture/wendell-e-berry-lecture.

6   G. Peter Winnington (2006) *The Voice of the Heart: the working of Mervyn Peake's imagination* (Liverpool: Liverpool University Press), pp5-27.

7   For two examples, see http://www.sbs.com.au/topics/life/relationships/article/2016/07/28/study-finds-reading-fiction-develops-empathy and https://www.researchgate.net/publication/264162058_The_greatest_magic_of_Harry_Potter_Reducing_prejudice, [accessed 9th February 2017].

Ruth EJ Booth is a BSFA award-winning fiction writer and academic, studying on the MLitt in Fantasy at the University of Glasgow. Her work can be found at www.ruthbooth.com

Reviews

The Corporation Wars:
Insurgence
Ken MacLeod
Orbit, 320 pages
Review: Iain Maloney

Midway through *Insurgence,*
the sequel to *Dissidence* and
midpoint of the trilogy, Carlos
the Terrorist finds himself in
a hellish maze, his way lit by
faint clumps of phosphorescent
lichen. He knows the path in
front of him will be difficult but
that his goal, everything he's
fought for in his life – and virtual
afterlife – is in this direction. It's
a computer generated simulation
based on a thousand-year-old
game popular when Carlos was
alive, a circle within a circle
within... well, it's still not clear
how deep it all goes. It may very
well be turtles all the way down.

The maze is a perfect metaphor
for the series. *The Corporation
Wars* are a labyrinth of reality

and unreality, lies, ruses, fictions
and double-double crosses that
would baffle even the smartest
AI, where you have just enough
information to keep you on
track but are lost in a web of
unanswered questions. Each
chapter brings a new development
that only redoubles the confusion.

Fortunately, we can trust the
architect. Ken MacLeod is a
master storyteller who makes
all this plot-based writhing
so enthralling that we forgive
the confusion. The scenarios
and characters introduced in
Dissidence return with a few
additions, most delightfully the
freebot known as Baser, who is
perfectly happy building a home
for itself on a solitary rock until
its peace is shattered by the
arrival of some noisy, aggressive
humans. The freebots are a
wonderful creation, sympathetic
and amusing characters coping

with their recent sentience.

The reader is clearly encouraged to side with the freebots against both human/AI factions, the Acceleration and the Reaction. The former are ultra-Capitalists, the latter far, far, far-right conservatives intent on a white supremacist future for mankind. Because of the wit with which MacLeod writes, each character is entertaining and compelling, even when you find their politics abhorrent, but there are no humans we could really term 'likeable'. The freebots however, well, them you can really identify with.

The centrepiece of the novel is the battle between a hardcore Acceleration faction and the Direction unit we were embedded with in *Dissidence*. Since nobody really knows which group really represents which faction and there are sleepers, traitors and those just plain fed up with the whole thing secreted in each team, it's almost impossible to set out, without the aid of multi-dimensional graphics, what happens in *Insurgence*. There are dramatic set-piece battles, tense escapes from captivity, epic drunken parties in a computer generated fantasy world, as much casual sex as you could ask for and, thankfully, a good few discussions and debates that expand the backstory and fill in some of the gaps in our understanding.

Many issues that will concern us in 2017, such as the return of far-right ideology and the prospect of AI revolutionising the workplace and economy, are played out and examined from a number of angles, though always within the demands of the storyline and without ever straying into dry

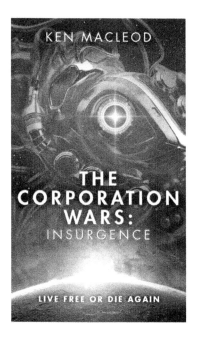

KEN MACLEOD

THE
CORPORATION
WARS:
INSURGENCE

LIVE FREE OR DIE AGAIN

philosophising. A key character is the logical conclusion of the right wing internet troll, whose hate speech made him an icon back in the day and who now considers himself a sleeper agent – though it's unclear if this is strategically valuable or just another piece of self-aggrandisement by an epic egotist. He balances on a razor's edge of ideology and self-interest, admitting to himself that a lot of what he espoused was nothing more than rhetoric while a battle, inspired in part by that rhetoric, unfolds around him.

Unlike many middle parts in a trilogy, this isn't merely a placeholder getting us from the beginning to the end. Rather it's a tight, startling thriller that builds on part one and sets up part three without ever taking its eye off the prize: walking us through that dastardly labyrinth in breath-taking, humorous style.

Thought X: Fictions and Hypotheticals
Edited by Dr Rob Appleby and Ra Page
Comma Press, 304 pages
Review: Pippa Goldschmidt

This volume is the latest in a series of anthologies published by Comma Press showcasing specially written short stories inspired by a specific theme. This one takes as its subject 'thought experiments', experiments carried out in the safety of one's own head to explore the world. Each short story is accompanied by an essay written by an expert in the field.

Thought experiments can be used to expose the apparent misconceptions of a theory and one of the most famous was devised by Schrödinger to clarify what he thought of as the wrong-headed interpretation of his own wave equation by other physicists. The cat trapped in a box who simultaneously exists in the quantum states and is both alive and dead until the box is opened was meant to be a *reductio ad absurdum,* an obviously impossible circumstance. In this anthology Schrödinger's cat is used inventively by Margaret Wilkinson in her story 'If He Wakes' to explore the complex relationship between an adult daughter and her father who may (or may not) be living in a nursing home.

That story succeeds because it's able to get beyond its inspiration and work as a short story in its own right, but not all the stories in this anthology manage to shake off their obvious starting point. Thought experiments share many characteristics with short stories, such as a reliance on a narrative which exploits the possibilities

THOUGHT X
Fictions & Hypotheticals

Edited by Rob Appleby & Ra Page

inherent in the set-up, and a reliance on an imagined world. And sometimes these shared characteristics seem to operate as an inhibitor. If a short story is also a thought experiment then can it sufficiently assert its own literary merits? Can a short story be more than a simple population of the underlying thought experiments with words? 'Lightspeed' by Adam Marek suffers from a workmanlike approach to its inspiration the Twin Paradox, in which an astronaut experiences the passage of time at a slower rate compared to the people left behind, and because of this he has problems with his marriage. But it's not wholly believable that this character wouldn't understand and be able to quantify the effect of time dilation on his domestic life.

In contrast, 'Red' by Annie Kirby takes the famous 'Mary's Room' experiment and turns it into something genuinely new. In the original experiment a young girl growing up in a monochrome world has an intellectual knowledge of the colour red, but apparently lacks a full understanding until she experiences it for the first time. This short story has the confidence to invert the main idea and isn't afraid to depart some distance from it. 'Monkey Business' by Ian Watson imagines those infamous monkeys randomly hitting typewriter keys and after some unpredictably long period of time, producing the entire works of Shakespeare. The fact that this thought experiment is so well-known could have acted as a disadvantage, but Watson manages to use his own narrative to extend our understanding of how the experiment might actually work.

'Keep It Dark' by Adam Roberts is a terrific imagining of a possible (and quite bonkers) answer to Olbers paradox—that apparently naïve question of why the sky is dark at night which has worried several centuries of astronomers and philosophers. The accompanying essay covers a lot of ground but presents the answer to the paradox a little too simplistically.

The essays vary in their technicality and there is a small amount of repetition across them, but it is fascinating to read about 'Mary's Room' by the man who actually came up with the idea. And it's also refreshing to see actual equations and diagrams in a book of stories. This makes for a lively mix of styles and subject matter. Comma are to be applauded for encouraging fiction writers to write (and readers to read) about such unusual topics.

Iraq +100: Stories from Another Iraq
Hassan Blasim (editor)
Comma Press, 224 pages
Review: Chris Kelso

A nation's literature is often shaped by historical and political events, and there aren't many countries who have recently undergone such immense turmoil and upheaval as Iraq.

It's funny: science fiction seems such an obvious genre to explore for a population which has suffered decades of oppression, censorship and violence – and yet, not many have. There are, of course, reasons for this – the government's dogged application of the 1969 penal code for one.

Iraqi+100, edited by controversial author/filmmaker Hassan Blasim, is an anthology which aims to overturn the Western world's preconceptions of what contemporary Iraqi literature is all about. He encourages his writers to shed the shackles of inflexible

religious discourse (which has restricted so much of Iraq's creative output over the years) and take a renewed pride in the Arab poetic tradition. In essence, this is a book about promoting progressiveness, and it's long overdue.

Blasim assembles some of the brightest among the young Iraqi diaspora and lets them run in any direction with his mission statement: Imagine your homeland in the year 2103, a century after the US/UK invasion. What we get is ten fascinating and courageous short stories that bend the allegory of the future into something poignant and relevant - one almost feels that *Iraqi +100* should be required reading for any super power.

The anthology opener really sets the tone, an introduction full of bitter irony. Anoud's 'Kahramana' starts with a young woman escaping her marriage to Mullah Hashish, leader of a group of anti-tech extremists called Empire (a faction which cleverly mirrors the real Islamic State) - but when she escapes one oppressive environment she finds herself quickly caught up in various others, each populated by tyrannical immigration officials and sensationalist television reporters who twist and distort Kahramana's story to suit their own agenda. It's a pertinent tale that resonates events closer to home – look no further than the French government's recent promise to close the UK border post in Calais post-Brexit.

Diaa Jubaili, the only writer still based in Iraq, portrays a grisly future in 'The Worker'. A portrait of a city which has been devastated by the loss of natural resources. The influence of faceless foreign corporations is another ever-present theme.

While most of the usual tropes are circumvented, there is the occasional foray into tried and trusted SF devices - virtual reality even makes an appearance in Jalal Hassan's 'The Here and Now Prison' and an intriguing alien invasion in 'Kuszib' by Hassan Abdulrazzak.

The fact of the matter is that the horror and cruelty goes on today, and the future doesn't look much brighter. Remember, we're still bombing this country. We played a part in turning Bagdad into this type of dystopian wasteland. It shouldn't take an anthology of fiction for that penny to drop, but if it does then the more the better.

The writing is superb and the stories are all beautifully executed, but it's difficult to read some of these stories. There is a collective shame that marinates the people of Britain after our government's decision to play a part in such an abominable act of senseless brutality. The whole book feels harrowing and necessary – for Westerners and Iraqi's alike.

Keep in mind that in Iraq, the sinister totalitarian governments of George Orwell or Philip K Dick novels are real, not science fiction. It's useful to have a reminder.

Invasion
Luke Rhinehart
Titan, 432 pages
Review: Chris Heyman

Earth is invaded by thousands of super-intelligent beach balls that want to play. This is the high concept that Luke Rhinehart uses to satirise modern economic ruts and wider social absurdities, as

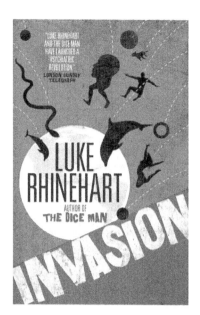

louche disconnect, and fittingly, subsequent novels struggled to match up. If this early peak wasn't enough to make me wary, I happen to be mildly prejudiced against the output of octogenarians. Rhinehart is 84. I'm flattered to say that he saw this coming, and rather than sending me a choice verb and pronoun, he creates a main character showing early signs of old age. This creates a bridge between writer and audience, to deliver an old man's view on a rapidly changing world. If you are in fact old, then I assume this is less of a conduit and more of a sympathetic character.

The said character is Billy Morton, who comes with a bitching wife and a couple of mischievous sons. He's a fisherman off Long Island, content with his relaxed lifestyle until a funny fish finds its way to him: Louie, the first of a handful of shape shifting invaders. These are the Ickies, hairy creatures of nigh infinite intelligence from another dimension who have arrived to teach the Earthlings a thing or two about fun. Their idea of 'fun' involves rambunctious protests, stage shows, hacking, theft and running for president. Chapters jump between multiple perspectives but it is Billy and his family that anchor the novel, giving it a heart. As the benevolent aliens suffer and die in the face of human evil we see the cost on a nuclear family as the modern media sets them on a pendulum swing between celebrity and terrorist.

As the activities of the invaders amps up, so too does the satire. Rhinehart's voice breezily unpicks economic fallacies as he tactfully suggests we might all be happier if we thought less about money

seen through the perennial trope of a fresh pair of eyes. Except that these balls have no eyes, just a shaggy coating of extra-sensory hair. It is to Rhinehart's credit that there are no gags about hairy balls until the very last page, a trailer for the next adventure. Indeed, taken at face value, this is the first of a series, and is left without resolution. Nonetheless, it's unusual for satire to invest in such a long game. The book's page count dwarfs the Vonnegut science fiction that is the closest comparison, yet doesn't feel too baggy. There are lots of really good ideas here and Rhinehart is not your stereotypical genre-jumping pensioner.

Rhinehart conquered the world of armchair psychologists in 1971 with The Dice Man, an electrifying debut that blurred the line between fiction and reality by chronicling the misadventures of one Luke Rhinehart. The book owed a debt to Joseph Heller's and politics, and more about having fun and helping people. It doesn't feel preachy, with warm humour and just a pinch of the ribald. In these interesting times things can date very quickly, but the political angle is vague and astute enough to cover the inclement weather of Washington DC. I'm excited to see Rhinehart finish his sequence and resolve a subtly harrowing cliffhanger.

The Cygnus Virus
TJ Zakreski
Dancing Star, 366 pages
Review: Steve Ironside

The search for life on another world is not without its risks. Some worry that we'll end up advertising our presence to a dangerous civilisation who'll come to enslave us; some worry the knowledge that we've contacted someone else will throw our own societies into disarray, and lead to the end of life as we know it. Or what if an alien intelligence were already among us, and then pops up in plain sight? How would we respond?

Moreover, what if a series of bizarre coincidences were to mean that this alien contact happened as the result of a great cosmic accident? *The Cygnus Virus* is born from just this notion. On the planet of Terra (spookily reminiscent of our own Earth), a depressed guy named Andron, reeling from personal tragedy, signs up to a SETI-like program on his computer, and manages to download a space-faring intelligence called Cygnus.

Sadly for Andron, this is only the first step on a road that will ultimately lead him on a personal journey he could scarcely have imagined as Cygnus turns him into his henchman, with plans to

use cloning and a couple of tricks from his home planet of "Earth" to convince everyone on Terra that he's the Second Coming. Along the way, Andron will make allies, be forced to make decisions that put his friends in harm's way, he'll leave his old life far behind in his quest to get out from under Cygnus' heel, and save the world from his diabolical plans.

Will Cygnus succeed or can Andron save the day? Well, obviously I won't give that away— suffice to say that when your opponent is a computer-based personality that can control the Internet you'll definitely have your work cut out for you.

It's this quandary that allows the deeper themes of the book to develop, and they are interesting. There's more than a hint of William Gibson and Iain M Banks here, as the story plays with concepts like trans-humanism, cyber-terrorism, the nature of humanity and immortality, and the lengths to which one will

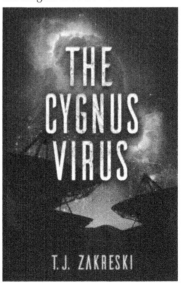

go for survival. Whereas those authors' worlds can be quite sterile, dystopian, disconnected places, Zakreski manages to keep the mood reasonably light, despite the darkness of a couple of the turns in the plot. While it's not a ha-ha-funny comedy, there's a streak of humour to be found.

Cygnus is at the heart of a cult of personality built on lies, manipulation and greed. His rise to power, linked to the Church of the Holy Cloth feels very much like the rise of populist movements today. If this review had been written nine months ago, it'd be chalked up as a cautionary tale – now, it can be viewed as a perfectly-timed work of clever observational satire.

The book's rhythm is great—the story flows along so well that I was half way through the book before it occurred to me that it was written in the present tense. I'm not a big fan of this technique, generally finding it cumbersome and that it gets in the way of the story, but I'm happy to have found an exception that proves my rule. It feels right—almost like a series of diaries, or a documentary show.

I enjoyed the characterisation in this tale as well—from Andron's beaten down yet still defiant outlook, to Cygnus' Rockstar delusions of godhood, the main characters in the story feel complete, and have great and distinctive voices. The folks that Cygnus manipulates to advance his plans have flaws that make them stereotypes that seem all too real in our new world of post-truth politics.

The only criticism I have is that there are storytelling tools that do not survive the trip through this tale either. The opening chapters,

with that documentary style, treat the events that set the story in motion as a kind of study in chaos theory. Once everything has been established, though, this whole external view is dropped. Given that this book is intended to be the first part of a trilogy, I wonder if this is something that will be picked up in later books. For now it just seems a strange way to approach the opening in comparison, but it's not ultimately damaging to the rest of the story, so it's more of a niggle than a complaint.

There are some clues as to how the planned trilogy may unfold, but given the generally completed story that this book delivers I'm intrigued by the possibilities. I'll certainly pick up part two to see how the story develops. *The Cygnus Virus* is a book that I would suggest picking up if the idea sounds in any way intriguing to you; given the times we live in, a book which plants its flag squarely in 'stick it to the man' territory with a side order of existential debate might be just the tonic that you need.

The Girl With Two Souls
Stephen Palmer
CSIPP, 378 pages
Review: Katie Gray

In Bedlam asylum, some time in the early twentieth century, Kora Blackmore wakes up. She eats her breakfast, chats with her nurse about her plans for the day, re-reads her only book – and receives a rare visitor, a mysterious stranger who calls himself Doctor Spellman. He leads her on a cunning escape, out of Bedlam, out of London, north to his family home in Sheffield, where he promises she'll be safe.

But as the title of the book

The Girl
With
Two Souls

"His work is unique, original, sometimes challenging, always fresh." Gary Dalkin, Amazing Stories

STEPHEN
PALMER

century fusing with the mass production of the industrial revolution to create a snowballing robotic workforce, given life by the mysterious 'soul giver'

Did Kora/Roka receive her extra soul from the soul giver? Did she suffer some form of mental break? Or is something stranger afoot?

Stephen Palmer weaves his clockpunk setting skilfully. Automata communicate with their masters through 'the lingua', a programming language written on a stenograph; their rise is having a devastating impact on the human workforce; already people are debating whether automata, like any other workers, deserve rights. The alternate timeline has a sense of realism; robots are woven seamlessly into real British history, looking back to the Luddites of the early nineteenth century and forward to contemporary fears of computerisation.

There are hints of larger, more fantastical things in the background. What (or who) is the soul giver? Doctor Spellman confesses that there's a dark secret at the heart of the factory and Sir Tantalus himself is frightened by his own work. All in all, it's an intriguing book, with plenty of questions left unanswered for future volumes.

But on the flip side, all those questions are part of the reason why *The Girl With Two Souls* left me a little cold. I wouldn't expect all the answers at the end of act one, but I was expecting some kind of a resolution. Instead the book rambles to a somewhat arbitrary stopping point. It feels more like act one of a long novel than volume one of a trilogy.

I'd happily read volume two—

suggests, he's rescued not one girl, but two. The next day, Roka Blackmore wakes in a strange bed in a strange house, confused and disoriented to find herself outside Bedlam. She, too, makes the acquaintance of Doctor Spellman—but is far less inclined than Kora to do as she's told…

Kora and Roka are two girls in one body. Together they're the illegitimate daughter of Sir Tantalus Blackmore, the genius behind the British automata workforce. While quiet, studious Kora investigates the mystery behind her curious condition and her father's work, strong-willed Roka stays up all night to see Lenin speak at a Communist rally, throws bricks through windows with the suffragettes—and champions rights for automata.

This alternate twentieth century is clockpunk rather than steampunk, the strange and unsettling automata of the eighteenth and nineteenth but to find out what happens, not because I'm especially invested in the characters. Neither Kora nor Roka is fleshed out enough for my liking. Far more attention is lavished on the differences between them than who either girl actually *is* as a person; Kora is quiet, studious and obedient, Roka is loud, illiterate and does as she likes. The contrast wears a bit thin. Hopefully both girls will be developed more in books to come.

Palmer is on thin ice with the inclusion of Bedlam and the ambiguity over Kora and Roka's condition. It should be self-evident, to any educated reader, that they don't have a natural illness as the situation depicted here is, quite simply, not how mental illness works. Dissociative Identity Disorder is a controversial, poorly-understood and stigmatised disorder, and in my opinion, it's a subject that writers of sci-fi and fantasy should stay well away from.

That said, the Bedlam scenes are brief and tasteful, Kora and Roka's condition renders them vulnerable rather than dangerous, and both are sure of their sanity and their status as separate people. Neither, refreshingly, is there any question of one of them being the 'real' girl; they're content to regard the other as an equal. As stories about multiple personalities go, this is a well-handled one, and I'd be surprised if later volumes reveal them to be one girl with a mental problem.

Overall, I had a good time reading *The Girl With Two Souls*. It's a fun read if you enjoy clockpunk aesthetic, with a plot that's rarely predictable and isn't afraid to get political. I look forward to reading the sequels

and I hope the resolution, when it comes, satisfies my curiosity.

Hold Back the Stars
By Katie Khan
Penguin Books/Doubleday Books
Review: Thom Day

Carys and Max are stuck in space. They've somehow managed to make it through the ring of meteors that surrounds Earth, but their spacecraft has been critically damaged in the process. Now with 90 minutes of oxygen left, they must fight to save each other and prove to the world below that the "utopian" rules governing Earth aren't as progressive and freeing as they seem.

I generally steer clear of the romance genre, but it's not often you get the opportunity to read romance set in a utopian post-war future, so I had to give *Hold Back the Stars* a go. It's a quick, fun read, and while it hasn't converted me to Mills & Boone, I

did find it surprisingly enjoyable.

It follows the standard girl-meets-boy storyline, but there's plenty of futuristic elements thrown in to keep non-romance readers intrigued. It's set in the near future, and opens with Carys and Max stranded outside their dying spacecraft with only 90 minutes of breathable air and no way to contact Earth. The story is split between their last hour and a half together and flashbacks to their burgeoning relationship.

Back on their future Earth, North America and the Middle East have devastated each other with nuclear weapons, and citizens of Europia—happily still including Britain—are Rotated every three years to different Voivodes to encourage cultural appreciation and understanding, and to discourage the possibility of future wars. Europia is governed by Representatives in the Grand Central Hall who uphold the rules of the new utopia, including the rule that serious relationships cannot be formalised (i.e. marriage) until both members are over 30. Carys and Max are in their early twenties, but Max's grandparents helped establish Europia and set up these rules, so his relationship with Carys threatens his bond with his family and challenges their entire way of life. Carys is an up-and-coming star in the space agency, so to prove the sincerity of their love to the Central Hall—and to Max's family—they are sent on a dangerous mission to find a way through the meteor field.

The science fiction is fun as long as you don't dig too deeply—I'm not sure the idea that Earth could capture a ring of meteors would hold up under astrophysical scrutiny—but it doesn't stand in the way of the story: it's a romance foremost with a good sci-fi background.

Meanwhile future Earth is an interesting place: Europia is a multicultural utopia, and united blocks exist around the globe, with Rotation occurring every three years. Aid is sent to the former United States, destroyed in a nuclear war with the Middle East, and people are encouraged to travel and learn other languages to increase cultural understanding. Hybrid electric vehicles are the norm, but space exploration has been halted by the meteor cloud now caught in Earth orbit. And there are sprayable bike locks—I don't know why I like this last detail so much, but it gives the story a great feeling of futuristic domesticity.

The romance itself is sweet, if stereotypically sappy, and Carys and Max are likeable, if stereotypically flawed, characters. Secondary characters are few and exist mainly to further the plot, but Max's friend Liu is a notable and refreshing exception.

Overall, *Hold Back the Stars* is an enjoyable, if not overly stimulating, story. The sci-fi elements held my non-romantic attention throughout, and any clunky writing could be mostly smoothed over by these elements. The ending left me disappointed, but this was mainly down to the story fitting the romance, rather than sci-fi, genre. Khan has a great imagination and paints a colourful, intriguing background for her characters to interact against, and I'd be interested to read more of her work in future.

Daughter of Eden
Chris Beckett
Corvus, Atlantic, 400 pages
Review: Iain Maloney

Daughter of Eden is the concluding part of a trilogy which began with Dark Eden and continued through Mother of Eden. 400 years have passed since Angela and Tommy were marooned on the strange world of Eden, and their descendants have bred, spread and developed. Eden's society is split into two main factions and when Daughter of Eden opens, war is literally on the horizon.

Angela Redlantern, whom we first met as the friend of Starlight in *Mother of Eden*, is the first to see the boats of the Johnsfolk bearing down on Mainground. She joins her family and neighbours as they flee over Snowy Dark to take refuge at the original landing ground, bringing the trilogy full circle.

I won't touch futher on the plot, to avoid spoiling the central premise of the narrative, beyond saying that it's a thrilling tale of cultural revolution, military conflict and something of a coming-of-age journey, though for a society rather than an individual. I have to admit to not being a fan of the middle instalment, *Mother of Eden*. The constantly shifting perspectives and patchwork narration were welcomingly original but the narrow focus on political machinations below ground in New Earth laboured under the weight of plot inevitability. Fortunately *Daughter of Eden* is a very different kind of book. The scope is much wider, drawing in the various groups from across Eden, and the two contrasted timelines Beckett shapes the novel around – the shocking present and the preparatory past where Angela is trained to become a shadowspeaker—a member of the Gela priesthood—give the story depth and dynamism lacking in *Mother of Eden*.

Beckett's work has long been fascinated with anthropology and cultural history, and the Eden trilogy wears its inspirations on the dust jacket. The first book explored a Cain and Abel-like story and how evil can be brought into the world. The second looked at how real events can become scriptural 'truths' that define a society and how one group can use these 'truths' to subjugate another, here through slavery and patriarchy. *Daughter of Eden* asks, "What happens when reality contradicts the 'truth' of these stories?" Eden truly is a paradise lost, but by playing the thought experiment through move by move, Beckett shows how humans can make a complete mess of things without the need for external malevolent

CHRIS
BECKETT

DAUGHTER OF EDEN

'A rising star of British SF... Beckett should be on
the radar of anyone who professes concern for science
fiction as a literary form' Alastair Reynolds

intervention. There are no serpents that side of the wormhole.

The bedrock of feminism on which the trilogy rests is also given a more nuanced airing in this novel. While *Mother of Eden* looked at the straightforward male-versus-female dynamic developing among the Johnsfolk, *Daughter of Eden* explores a female-versus-female dynamic in the struggle between the cynical shadowspeaker Mary and the naïve Angela. It is a truism that members of oppressed groups are often unwittingly complicit in their own oppression, but Mary's eagerness to preach whatever suits the headmen of Eden in order to protect her own power base, and her rage at being found out by Angela, give colourful life to the concept.

Despite being so overtly political and philosophical, *Daughter of Eden* avoids didacticism. Although the tone of all three novels is one of disapproval of religion, and organised religion in particular, the chaos caused by the dismantling of a belief system is sensitively handled, and the inevitable push-back and Trump-esque denial of reality is all too believable. When your entire existence is predicated on a particular understanding of the universe, it takes enormous strength and objectivity to abandon it. As Beckett shows us in Daughter of Eden, and recent events in reality underline, not everyone possesses those attributes.

The books are a great feat of world building that avoids all the usual cliches and pitfalls. Apart from a short section at the beginning of Daughter of Eden, exposition and explanation are kept within the action and are tied to plot developments, proving that the pages and pages of background given by lazier science fiction and fantasy writers can be dealt with in a more sophisticated manner. The language of Eden, developed from the childish English of the original first generation Edeners (Edenites? Edenonians?) is also a lesson for other world-builders in how small shifts in register or emphasis can render a known language unfamiliar. Edenese comes to life not in lists of new nouns and verbs that require an extensive glossary, but in the metaphors and similes drawn directly from the landscape of Eden.

The trilogy is a triumph of storytelling and a testament to the power of the novel form to explore what it means to be human. Beckett has created a coherent and enclosed world and there is definite scope for more stories from Eden, for this to develop into a longer series that studies human social development in a way reminiscent of Asimov's Foundation, while eschewing galaxy-wide panorama for a crucible. The Eden trilogy, like The Holy Machine before it, is what science fiction excels at: deconstructing complex ideas through the medium of compelling characters and captivating stories. Religion is both dangerous and necessary, as Marx pointed out, and here Eden is no different from Earth.

Parabolic Puzzles

Paul Holmes

The Rigellian Rugby Final

The day of the Big Match had finally arrived. The Rigellian planetary team had a huge advantage as the game was played to their rules. But the Earth team had some giants of the Union game, including Skinny Wooljinn, John Mualo, Eric Chicmaw and Haggis van Snit.

The whistle blew. There arose a tremendous hooting from the Rigellian contingent, while the Earthlings managed a spirited rendition of *Globe of Hope and Glory*. Rousing stuff!

Earth were the first to score a try, with a storming run up the left wing by Mualo, unceremoniously bashing Rigellians out of his way, but Rigel returned the favour in minutes. It was going to be close.

At half time the score was the product of two odd primes to Earth with Rigel just a whisker ahead on a fourth power.

The lead changed hands repeatedly throughout the tense match until the scores were level with one minute remaining. Encamped in the Rigellian half but repelled by a desperate and effective defence, there was only one option. The ball was thrown back to Wooljinn, but the Rigellians were hurtling towards him so quickly that he had no choice but to pass back to Haggis van Snit for a last-ditch drop-goal from the half way line.

The crowd hushed as the ball rose in a graceful arc, spinning and tumbling through the air. All the players fell silent, too, watching in awe as the oval ball made its way slowly towards the posts. Earthlings gasped as it seemed that the ball was going to fall short. After an eternity, the ball struck the bar and ricocheted into the air. This was too much to bear. The Rigellian crowd started blowing with all their might to try to affect its trajectory.

To no avail. It finally descended between the posts, and the stadium erupted. Earth had won the Invitation Cup for the first time in its history. The final score: Earth—a square and triangular number; Rigel—the sum of the first four factorials.

What were the scores at Half Time and Full Time? And who were the anagramised rugby players?

Send your answer to us via our website Contact Form. If you are correct, your name will be dropped into a hat. A copy of Paul Holmes' book **The Galactic Festival** *will be sent to the lucky name pulled out of said hat.*

Paul's latest collection of Puzzles, *The Galactic Festival* has just been published by Shoreline of Infinity Publications.
Available from www.shorelineofinfinity.com and from bookshops worldwide.

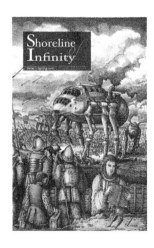

How you can Help

Thank you for buying this issue of Shoreline of Infinity: your purchase goes towards the fees we pay our writers and artists, and towards the costs of running the magazine.

Thank you too for reading this issue of Shoreline of Infinity: by so doing the writers, artists and the editorial team— and we hope you do too—receive a warm fuzzy feeling inside.

As you sit with us around the fire of driftwood, sparks floating to mingle with the stars in the sky, can we ask you do one more small thing? Can we ask you to sponsor Shoreline of Infinity SF magazine?

Here are some of the ways you can do that, and the benefits for you:

Esteemed Reader $1 per month	Hallowed Holder of the Book $5 per month	Potent Protector of the Printed Word $10 per month	Mighty Mentor of the Masterpiece $40 per month
Digital subscription to Shoreline of Infinity quarterly	Print edition subscription to Shoreline of Infinity quarterly	Sponsorship of one story in Shoreline per year	Sponsorship of one Shoreline cover picture per year
Get your copy of Shoreline before the general public sees it	Free postage and packing	The Patron's name published with the story	The Patron's name appears prominently on the back cover
Access to patron-only updates from the Shoreline team	Plus all previous rewards	A certificate identifying the Patron as the sponsor of the story, naming the story and the writer	A high quality print of the cover image suitable for framing
Exclusive access to the Shoreline private forum		Plus all the benefits of an Esteemed Reader	Plus all the benefits of an Esteemed Reader
Your name in our hall of heroes on the Shoreline website		Plus all the benefits of a Hallowed Holder of the Book	Plus all the benefits of a Hallowed Holder of the Book

And there's more. Visit our Patreon page:

www.patreon.com/shorelineofinfinity

And find out how you can help.

Shoreline of Infinity founders
Noel Chidwick, Editor
Mark Toner, Art Director
Edinburgh, Scotland